Mixed-up Doubles

Mixed-up Doubles

BY

ELENA YATES EULO

HOLIDAY HOUSE / *New York*

Printed in the United States of America
www.holidayhouse.com
First Edition

Library of Congress Cataloging-in-Publication Data

Eulo, Elena Yates.
Mixed-up doubles / by Elena Yates Eulo.—1st ed.
p. cm.
Summary: With the help of an unlikely new friend, ninth grader Hank tries to adjust to his parents' recent divorce and works toward his dream of being a successful tennis player.
ISBN 0-8234-1706-9
[1. Tennis—Fiction. 2. Divorce—Fiction. 3. Friendship—Fiction.] I. Title.

PZ7.E869 Mi 2003
[Fic]—dc21
2002069093

For my son, Kenny—
In whose creative mind
Hank and his friends were born.
With love and
admiration.

1

Alamar, California. My new hometown is about the size of an anthill.

I hate everything about this place. A "seaside" town, Dad called it. From our house, you can't see even a puddle of ocean. I figured out that being this far away from the beach means we live on the wrong side of town.

Dad had a lot to say about that when I told him. For instance, that there is no wrong side of town. That being closer to the beach might be nice, but you might find the biggest tree or the most interesting restaurant or the kindest person thousands of miles away from the ocean.

"If that's true," I said, "why don't we go a thousand miles away from this place?"

He said, "Listen, Hank, go throw a Frisbee or something."

“I don’t have any dog to throw a Frisbee to,” I reminded him. “And you can’t say I’m not old enough to take care of one anymore. I’m starting the ninth grade. I could take care of ten dogs.”

He looked at me for a minute, then said, “I’m sorry about the ocean and I’m sorry about the dog. I’m sorry about everything, Hank.”

The truth is he made me feel guilty for being steamed that I came more than a hundred miles from L.A. to live on the wrong side of town.

Nothing’s gone right since the divorce. My parents are the only ones happier. Everything feels all wrong. I miss my old home and my old friends. If I have to admit it, I also miss our mom, and I don’t get how she and Dad think they can “share” us like they plan on doing. She gets summers and all vacations. He gets the rest of the time because she travels so much. Mom has promised to spend every minute she’s not on the road with her tennis clients visiting us.

Plus, she calls every day and always sounds like she’s got a cold when she hangs up. In between hello and good-bye, she begs my older brother and me to keep practicing our tennis. We promise we’ll go straight out to the court when we get off the phone, but we’re all talk. We haven’t even looked for a court.

Jerome hates tennis now. And every time he and Mom get into a fight, he hates it even more. If it hadn't been for tennis, he said, she'd have stayed home more and Dad wouldn't have wanted a divorce.

"What was I supposed to do?" she said. "Give up my career? Is that what you want?"

"Your career ruined our whole family," Jerome told her.

Used to be, any day was a great day if Jerome had a good tennis game on his schedule. These days, he'd pass up an invitation to the U.S. Open. He hasn't picked up a racket since we moved to Alamar.

I picked up one once. I threw it into the highest tree I could find. The tree happened to belong to the people next door, which is how I met this kid, Tremont. The racket knocked down a bird's nest, which about drove Tremont nuts. He's got this thing about not harming any living creature. The way he was screaming at first, I thought we'd moved next door to a bunch of barn owls on a night hunt. Then he figured out the nest was deserted and that the little pieces of blue eggs inside the nest were already broken from when the baby birds hatched out last spring.

Tremont is every bit as strange as his name. He's strange right down to his outie belly button. If I had something on me that looked like that, I'd hack it off with a penknife. But Tremont goes around without a shirt, and his shorts always fasten right under that ugly little thing. The rest of him is no beauty either. He's short and chunky, with strange feet. He walks like a gorilla. One of these days, someone is going to offer Tremont a banana.

"What do I call you?" I asked him. "Tree? Monty? What?"

He bunched up his face. "Tremont."

"The whole thing?"

"You can't remember all of it?"

He wanted to call me Harold until I told him that unless he called me Hank, he'd find himself up in a tree, not my tennis racket. After that, he never gave me any trouble.

In fact, he tried to get friendly. He asked me a lot of those dumb get-acquainted questions, like "Where did you come from? What kind of movies do you like? Do you like to play video games?" And what must have been the most important question, judging from the look on his face: "How come you wear such expensive sneakers? They look cool, don't get me wrong, but Mom says it's a rip-off to pay that much."

I skipped all the other questions and answered the last one. "My mom is a tennis coach. She won't let any of us wear anything but the best shoes. She says your game is in your feet as much as in your arm."

He studied my new air-cushioned, ventilated Nikes and muttered, "They're a rip-off, all right." Just the way he was standing there, legs buckled, toes together, made his feet look ashamed of themselves.

Tremont was different from the other neighborhood kids I'd met. He was the only guy on the block who didn't have that suspicious glare in his eye when he looked at me—like we both liked the same girl or were trying out for the same spot on the team. Of course, Tremont probably didn't have many girls or teams in his life. Unless maybe it was the debate team, and if it was, he must have figured out I'd be no competition.

It didn't take a rocket scientist to realize that if I started hanging around with someone like Tremont, he was definitely going to cramp my style.

"How old are you?" I asked.

"Fourteen. I'll be fifteen in March. Why?"

"You're sort of old for your age, aren't you?" I said. The truth was, he seemed about forty.

He shook his head. "Don't do that," he said.

"Don't do what?"

"That kind of thinking. That's jock thinking.

One-upmanship kind of stuff. It won't hold true in the real world, you know."

"Tremont, I hate to tell you, but we're in the real world."

"I meant part of the working world, not just starting high school," he said. "People like me are going to be the ones other people work for sooner or later."

"Like that isn't one-upmanship."

He laughed. "I have to admit it, Hank. You've got a point."

Now he really had me off balance. No kid ever tells another kid he's got a point that easy. Usually, you've got to be yanked out of the classroom by the principal before you tell that to each other. At least, that's been my own personal experience.

"Well, I'll be seeing you," Tremont said. "I feel like having a marshmallow and peanut butter sandwich." He shuffled toward his back door.

Just what he needs, I thought. In fact, that's what his body looked like in those white shorts with the elastic band cutting under his tan belly. A marshmallow and peanut butter sandwich.

At the screen door, Tremont looked back. "Sooner or later, Hank, we're going to have to be friends, you know. It's sort of inevitable, us living next door to each other and all. Gotta go with the flow. That's what my mom always says."

"Oh, sure," I said, talking to the ground. "We'll be friends."

"I mean the kind of friends that hang out together, Hank."

"Uh . . ."

He shook his head again. "Do yourself a favor, Hank. Don't be a walking cliché."

"A cliché of what?"

"Of a dumb jock. I mean, I know from looking at you you're a jock, but you sure as heck don't have to be a dumb one. My mom always says—"

"Stop quoting your mom, Tremont. That's about as embarrassing as it gets."

His shoulders heaved. "Okay." But I could just hear him thinking: Gotta go with the flow.

Then those big feet of his in their cheap sneakers flapped through the door and he disappeared inside the house.

"If I were you, I'd stay away from the peanut butter!" I yelled.

A strange kind of silence came over the place. It was as though Tremont had just frozen in midaction with one hand on the peanut butter and the other on the marshmallow bag. It wasn't barn owls that lived next door; it was Alfred E. Neuman.

Welcome to Alamar, I thought. Whoopee.

Tremont is horrible. Our house is horrible, tiny,

all brown-colored shingles, with a mud yard that Dad is starting to fertilize, lugging out bags of steer manure as if he really knows what he's doing. We'll be lucky to get a crop of crabgrass.

The school looks like a prison, and I start in there next week. Ninth grade for me, but my brother is a big cheese this year. A senior, which means Jerome's stuck in Alamar for only one school year. Then he'll go either to college on a tennis scholarship or straight into the pro circuit, which is what Mom wants him to do. He's *ready,* she says. She knows what she's talking about, because she's one of the top pro coaches. What she doesn't know is that if Jerome doesn't start practicing soon, he'll be lucky to play tennis in college, much less go pro. But what Mom doesn't know won't hurt her, my brother says with a wicked gleam in his eye.

Our little sister, Sarah, is going into kindergarten. She's the only one who's looking forward to going to school, but what she'd like better than anything is to go live with Mom. She cried in Dad's lap last night and told him so, and Dad said, "Look, honey, I have the stable situation."

And Sarah looked up at him and said, "Stable? You mean like horses?"

Jerome and I couldn't stop laughing.

There hasn't been much to laugh at lately, if you rule out Tremont's belly button, and with school coming at us next week, we'll be lucky if we laugh again before winter break.

"Don't sweat it," Tremont told me the next time I saw him. "Unless you're unlucky enough to get the Witch, you'll get good teachers. It's only her that's the horror."

Because I was curious about the school, I ended up talking to him for about an hour before I realized he thought we were building a friendship; then I starting edging away. I was looking for an excuse to get out of his backyard when Jerome yelled for me.

"I'm supposed to help unpack," I mumbled.

"Anything I can do to help?" Tremont asked from behind me.

I turned back. "That's the kind of stuff your mom used to ask your kindergarten teacher. Cut it out!"

"Okay. No problem."

"And stop being so nice about it. When I insult you like that, you tell me to get stuffed."

"Okay. Get stuffed."

No insult could reach the guy. He couldn't be for real. But for some reason I couldn't keep from laughing as I started lugging boxes around.

* * *

For the rest of the week, we unpacked and did what Dad called "settling in." Jerome has his own bedroom, and Dad made the largest bedroom into two rooms for Sarah and me. My room is the biggest and Sarah's is tiny, but cute with shelves for dolls on all sides. I walk past my sister's room to get to mine and there's always a night-light on now, even though just before the divorce, she'd learned to sleep in the dark.

Sometimes in the middle of the night, I can hear Sarah crying on the other side of the wall. I tiptoe in and sit on her bed and try to comfort her. But living in a new house without Mom is just too hard for her. She lies there with her head on her stuffed rabbit's stomach and cries until the bed shakes and both she and her rabbit are soaked in tears.

I guess we all look like a pathetic sight. Jerome all unsmiling and not talking much. Sarah crying all the time. Me with a hole in my heart. Everybody's clothes are wrinkled, even the stuff that is supposed to be wrinkle-free. It's a good thing nobody ever feels hungry because Dad is a sorry cook. Nothing seems to matter.

On the first day of school, Tremont knocked on my door bright and early.

"I've come to walk to school with you," he said, as if he was doing me a favor.

"Thanks," I said. "It's more than four blocks. I was afraid I might get lost."

He just grinned and waited for me to get my notebook. "Make sure your pencils have good erasers on them," he said.

I glared at him. "Erasers? I do all my work in pen. And never get a smudge."

His eyes said he doubted it. You'd think the wiseacre could see those two six-packs of erasers I'd just stuck in my backpack.

I was thinking of how to ditch this loser when Dad looked at me from behind his paper. Being as old as he was, it was obvious he'd forgotten all he ever knew about the stigma of going to your first day of school walking alongside a total social disaster. I knew what I had to do. A block from school, I'd suggest a race to the front steps and take off. I'd be inside the school and lost in the crowd before Tremont even got to the first step.

Of course, we weren't even half a block from home when kids came from everywhere, all heading in the same direction. Most of them, I could tell, were smirking at me walking along with Tremont. Oh, yeah. You could just feel the smirking. It was worse than walking along with a piece of toilet paper stuck to your shoe. I hadn't even gotten to school yet, and I was already ruined.

Naturally, I got the Witch for homeroom and Algebra 1, which was going to be my worst subject if the eighth grade pre-algebra class I took last year was any kind of clue. Miss Caster is the Witch's real name, and she wears purple lipstick and puckers her lips so that her mouth looks like a juicy grape getting ready to explode. Her whole world is algebra. You could ask the Witch which is worse—a megaton meteorite heading straight for Alamar or a D on your algebra test—and it wouldn't even be a contest. The algebra test would kill her every time.

Tremont got the Witch, too. Because the school is so small, they don't have enough staff for honors classes in ninth grade. Tremont is a born curve buster if I ever saw one.

"Don't worry," he said, taking the desk right behind mine. "If we do good work, the Witch will love us."

"Oh, boy," I said without looking back at him. "My heart is thrilled."

Algebra is easy, Tremont wrote on a piece of paper, and passed it to me.

Algebra is a disease, I wrote back.

The Witch gave us a basic skills test to see if any of us had actually learned anything in pre-algebra. On the way home, Tremont said the test was so easy, a child of five could have passed it. He asked me what I thought about the test.

I said, "A chocolate chip cookie, that's how easy it went down." That's something my mom says. Now that she's not with us, I quote her a lot. Not that I'd tell that to Tremont.

"By the way," he said, "Nick Lutazzi asked me if you were going to paint your house."

"What did you say?"

"I told him I thought you were too poor to paint it. He thought that sounded right. He said why else would you have moved into a brown house without painting it first?"

I would have kicked Nick Lutazzi's butt if he didn't have a really big one. I mean a big two-hundred-pound one. Nick was going out for offensive guard on the JV football team. If his shoulders being as wide as an apartment complex counted for anything, he had it made.

"Tell Nick Lutazzi," I said, "that my family's got this thing about brown houses. We love 'em. Me, I've always dreamed about living in one, but I never thought my dream would come true."

"Yeah, right," Tremont said. He picked a falling purple jacaranda leaf from out of the air and stared at it like he'd struck it rich. He put it against his cheek and stroked it until it gave me a queasy feeling.

I gritted my teeth at him. "You're getting weird on me, Tremont."

He ducked his head and stuck the leaf into his pocket. "I am?"

"It comes natural to you."

A big sigh came out of him. That was the first time I understood how much being weird bothered Tremont. Then he shrugged, as if he didn't have much choice but to accept it.

"Hank," he said, "before you moved in, everybody on our block was just hoping and praying that somebody would move into that ratty old brown house who could afford to paint it and fix it up. While it was vacant, some kids used to sneak inside it and play like it was haunted. I just thought you should know."

"Gee, thanks, bud."

"And you know when your dad does his gardening? Half the neighborhood goes out to watch him. It's funnier than watching june bugs in January. Doesn't your dad know anything about fertilizer and stuff? Take my word for it, Hank, nothing's going to grow on his lawn. He can water it until the year two thousand ten. Even weeds couldn't survive in your dad's lawn."

Well, so far, I'd told Tremont he was weird and he'd told me our family was an embarrassment to the whole block. We were off to a good beginning.

"How come your mom never comes to visit?" Tremont asked.

"How come your dad never comes to visit?" I said.

That's something else we shared: divorce.

"Want to do algebra homework together?" Tremont offered.

"That easy stuff? I'll be finished with it in ten minutes."

"Me, too. Let's get a snack and meet in your backyard in a half hour."

Oh, boy, I thought. Now when am I going to get my algebra homework done?

That night, my brother, my sister, my dad, and I all sat around the living room like we'd been through a demolition derby. My dad said he was so beat that even his eyelashes hurt. Not only had he gotten us all up at daybreak and fixed us breakfast and made our lunches, but he and Jerome had had to help Sarah and me get all our stuff together and get Sarah into some school clothes. Then Jerome went to the high school main campus and I went to the ninth-grade center and Dad took Sarah to kindergarten. She cried and wouldn't let go of him, and when she finally did, he was late for his new accounting job. Then after he got home from work and cooked dinner and he and Jerome did dishes, he still had to fill out papers that all three of us brought home from school. Papers on everything from medical release forms to emergency numbers.

"I wish Mommy was here," Sarah said, crying. She was so little and cute that even her tears were little and cute. They looked like shiny beads trickling down her cheeks.

Jerome took Sarah onto his lap and patted her on the head like she was a puppy.

I looked at Dad. "How come I have to take my lunch to school? Everyone but me buys. And you put my lunch in a baby lunch box. I threw it in the trash can."

Dad sighed. "I'm sorry, Hank. Your mother was right. There are some advantages to having a housekeeper. I'm not used to lunches. It'll get better."

"I'll buy."

"You'll buy. How much is the damage?"

"One fifty for a hamburger, chips, and drink. Two dollars for a hamburger and fries."

"For now, you'll go with the chips."

About then, the phone rang. It was Mom. She said, "How was school?" like she was expecting us to say it was the most wonderful thing since French toast. I looked at Jerome holding his extension and saw he wasn't going to say anything, so I said, "It was okay."

"Okay?" our mother said. "Just *okay*?"

"On a scale of one to ten?" I asked while Jerome just sat there. "It was a . . . ah . . ." It wasn't even on the scale.

"It was a four," I told her. It sounded high to me.

"A *four,*" Mom kept repeating.

"Or even higher."

"Jerry?" Mom said. "Are you there?"

"Yeah, Mom. I'm here."

"Have you been practicing your serve every day?"

"Oh, sure." My brother rolled his eyes at me. "Absolutely. I even practice when it rains. I ruin a lot of balls that way." He pushed his horn-rims higher up on his nose, and they fell right back again.

These days, Jerome was looking more like a nerd than Tremont. He was even combing his hair like Tremont. He leered into the phone when Mom bought the lie about all the practicing he was doing.

“And are you fantastic like always?” Mom asked in that eager voice that just bubbled over with pride. Jerome, she had always told us, had everything it took to be a major star on the circuit.

Jerome gave one of those horrible grins. “Oh, yeah, Mom, I’m sort of amazing, all right. In fact, you wouldn’t know me.”

“That’s great,” she said. “Hank? How’s your game? You’re going to be a star, too, like your brother, you know.”

I hope not, I thought. Not if it means parting my hair down the middle and wearing black horn-rims. But I said, “Well, I keep plugging.”

Actually, I had a secret dream of being a pro, too, like Jerome. I’d never mentioned it to anybody, not even Mom. For as long as I could remember, I’d been my brother’s volley partner, and I’d just about crawl off the court when he’d finished slamming balls at me. Every single time I thought about going pro, I ended up telling myself, Hank, you’re pretty good for a kid your age, but you’ll never be as good as Jerome, not in a thousand years, no matter what Mom says. Why dream of something you’ll never get?

Jerome was better at school than me, and he had all the talent for tennis that I’d always wanted to boot, and here he was, just throwing it away. And Mom didn't even know it, that's how out of our lives she was these days.

She was in Florida right now, she said, coaching one of the top seeds in a tournament in Miami, but she'd be back in California next weekend and she'd see us then.

"I love you," she kept saying. "Well . . . take care of yourselves, okay? Promise me?"

I said, "Sure, okay." But I was thinking, Why aren't you here to take care of us yourself? Answer that.

Mom sighed. "I'll call you tomorrow night and see how everything's going," she said. "Maybe it'll be better tomorrow, right?"

Jerome said nothing, and Sarah said even less.

"Right," I said. As oldest kid, Jerome had dibs on wearing the biggest chip on his shoulder. As the youngest, Sarah couldn't say too much. That left me as middleman. Mr. Peacemaker. "Don't worry; we're okay," I told her.

"Well . . . bye then," she said in a shaky voice. "Don't forget . . . I love you guys a lot."

"Love you, too," I mumbled. The pit of my stomach dropped to my kneecaps.

When we hung up, nobody could think of one

thing to say, not even Dad. Especially since Sarah was in his lap, crying too hard to talk. Jerome just got up and left the room.

There are times like this when I get so mad at Mom for not being here that I think: Just stay away for good. Who needs you?

It was after midnight when a thumping sound woke me up, like pounding blood in my brain.

Thump . . . thump . . . thump.

Now what? I thought. An egg attack, to make us paint the house?

But this thumping was louder than egg throwing, even hard-boiled eggs. I'd heard this sound for as long as I could remember. I knew it better than my own heartbeat.

Jerome, I thought.

I got out of bed and looked down over the cracked driveway. A light was turned on over the garage door, and there he was, smashing tennis balls against it.

I got goose bumps just watching him.

Even volleying a ball off a garage door in the middle of the night in a town nobody ever heard of, my brother was something to see.

That *whack, whack, whack* was sharper and cleaner than an ax cutting wood. His game was in his legs, his feet, his arms. The slant of his body. Even his head drove the ball.

Nobody could play like that and not love it.

He was exploding now, sending the ball careening in all directions, and I swear he was the only person I could imagine who could return his own ball.

Wham, wham, wham!

He poured on the steam, never missing a beat. And then all of a sudden, he just quit. The ball flew past him, rocketing down the driveway and into the street.

Jerome leaned over, both hands on his knees, his right hand still holding the racket. His shirt was stuck to his back. He looked like he'd just lost the most important game of his life.

And me . . . well, I don't think I've ever been as sad in my life as I was that night, looking out of my window, staring down at my brother.

Finally, he stood up, took a deep breath, and straightened his back. He looked down at the racket in his hand, and then he let it fall like it wasn't even worth throwing away. He walked toward the house, and he never looked back.

The next morning, I got up early and carried the racket inside. If it hurt to think of Jerome giving up tennis, it hurt even more to think of his best racket lying there waiting to get run over by a car.

I put the racket with mine and I thought, I'll give it to him when he changes his mind and wants to play again.

Or was it possible that he'd really finished with tennis?

I didn't know.

After class on Friday, Miss Caster said, "Hank, I'd like to see you for a few minutes."

Just the words I needed to hear. The ax had fallen.

Sure enough, when everybody else had run out the door, she pulled out a pile of my papers marked all over with red ink.

"I'm afraid we're having some trouble," she said.

"What kind of trouble are we having?" I asked. I stared at the papers. If the red ink she'd used to correct the papers with had been blood, there would have been enough for a transfusion.

The Witch gave me a suspicious look because of the "we" stuff I'd thrown back at her. She shoved the whole stack of my work at me.

Okay, Hank, old buddy, I said to myself. So what if you made a few mistakes? Keep a stiff upper lip.

Remember, you can't let the Witch think she's getting to you or it'll be all over for you.

"Hank? Are you examining your work?"

"Yes, ma'am. I'm looking it all over."

I really was, and I was thinking she'd even put her red marks over some good work. Why would she mark a whole algebra problem wrong when all I did was accidentally leave out two steps of the danged thing? It was a clear case of her hating me, just like everyone else hated me. Like the PE kickball captain choosing me last for the team in Sports 1. Even Tremont got picked before me. I felt like yelling at the fools: "I'm an athlete!" Which I was glad I didn't, because I kicked out my first and only time up. It only went to show what a bogus class Sports 1 was. Kickball. In high school yet!

"You can do much better work than this, Hank," the Witch said.

"I was feeling a little sick last Monday when I took my test," I told her.

"This is a week's worth of work."

"I was sick all week."

Miss Caster gave me one of those wise teacher looks over the top of her glasses and said, "Hank, what's going on?"

"I hate school, that's all." I was counting the veins in her nose.

She thought about that for a minute, and then said, "All school, or just my class?"

Oh, boy, what an opportunity, I thought. Then I sighed and let it go by. This is the way teachers set you up. Then when you fall into their trap, they make you pay. And pay.

"All school," I mumbled.

"How about recess?" she said.

"Especially recess," I told her. "I hate it all. Everything." Especially her. If I'd had a glass of water handy, I'd have poured it on her head to see if she'd melt like the Wicked Witch of the West.

"You're going to learn," she said, "that this kind of attitude isn't going to get you far. Especially in my class."

Tremont was waiting for me in the hallway. He must be the toughest human being in the world to get rid of. In his next lifetime, he'll probably come back as a wad of gum on somebody's shoe.

"So, what did the Witch want?" he said. "She failing you already?"

"Heck, no, man. She wants to give me a special award for general excellence in everything. She even likes my handwriting."

Mr. Goody Two-shoes, who had gotten straight one hundred percents and had his name written up on the blackboard, fell into step with me as if we always walked home together. Okay, so we always did. I had fallen into that terrible habit. With Tremont running after me like a dog and everybody calling us best buddies and laughing up their sleeves about it, what difference did it make? I was already ruined.

"You're failing algebra already, aren't you?" he asked.

"How can I be failing when we're just beginning, Tremont? I thought you were supposed to be a brain."

"If you see the beginning of an equation," Tremont said in his superior way, "you can start to get clues as to the conclusion."

We walked along toward home, me strutting tall, Tremont bobbing along at my shoulder. One of us dumb, one of us a brain. Sure enough, we were starting to seem like old friends, the way we never gave each other a break.

"There's only one thing to be done," he said. "I'm going to have to be your tutor."

Cold sweat broke out all over my body. Tremont, my tutor. Before I stooped to that, I'd get F minuses in everything. Let them invent a new mark for how lousy I was. Let them put me back in second grade.

"Not a chance," I said.

"It's done," Tremont said. "We'll go straight home and hit the old books."

"I can't do it on an empty stomach."

"We'll eat first. My mom always leaves tuna fish or lunch meat or something."

"Uh, Tremont . . ."

"And home-baked cookies and mint chocolate chip ice cream . . ."

"I just don't think it's going to work out."

"You can have a microwave pizza. The freezer's full of them."

I hadn't seen a pizza of any variety since we moved to Alamar and started living on a shoestring. The house took all of Dad's money, and he wouldn't take a penny from Mom, except for child support. It was a point of honor, he said. Especially since he was the one to decide on the divorce. Not that Mom had made any objections.

I took a big bite of the inevitable and said, "Tremont, you're on. Just don't wear purple lipstick."

Our first session was too horrible to talk about. Tremont said I wasn't concentrating, but he was wrong. I was concentrating on how much I hated algebra.

"I think I'm blocked," I told him.

By the time we were finished, I was ready to bang tennis balls off the garage door for the first time since I'd moved to Alamar. I slammed them as hard as I could slam them, first with my forehand, then with my backhand. I slammed them so long and so hard, I was surprised the garage still had a door. When I was done, I stood there sweating and looking at the dead ball in my hand.

And feeling pretty good. It's crazy how I always feel better when I'm playing tennis.

"Pretty awesome," Tremont said, coming over from his backyard with his algebra book under his arm. "You are a great athlete, Hank."

"I'm nothing, compared to my brother," I said.

"Who's comparing?" Tremont said. He grinned at me. "Now that you've got all that stuff out of your system, maybe we can get down to studying some algebra."

"We've done algebra," I said.

"No, we haven't," he said. "Not really."

I don't know how he talked me into it, but we ended up back at the kitchen table with the algebra book open between us. Somehow, a few of those hieroglyphics started to make a little sense.

"Don't go thinking you know anything yet," Tremont warned me after I'd gotten one problem right. "You're still about the dumbest jock I know."

I looked him up and down. "Tremont," I said, "if you're going to teach me algebra, I'm going to teach you tennis. But don't go thinking you're ever going to be any good. You're about the lamest physical specimen I ever set eyes on."

"Wow," he said. "I'm getting free tennis lessons from the best tennis player I ever saw outside of the pros."

He grinned.

"Don't think I don't know you're getting in your digs, Hank," he said. "But I'm not letting you off the hook about those tennis lessons. Let's start right now."

We went back outside and hung a string across the driveway to act as the net. Then I started the sorry job of teaching him the basics. Like holding a racket. He held it out in front of him like he was tossing flapjacks in a frying pan.

"You're the worst I ever saw," I told him.

"So? You do algebra like I swing a tennis racket," he said.

I saw his point. Fact is, I had to laugh. He did, too.

Mom picked us up that Saturday at one. She was suntanned and thin, like always, and looking good, like always. For a while, it was as if we were all strangers, even when she hugged us. Sarah shrank back a little, and Mom got tears in her eyes then.

She was on her knees next to Sarah, and she looked up at Dad and said, “I’ve got to stop going on these meets. I’ve got to see them more.”

“And do what?” he said. “Give up all that money? I doubt that, Carolyn. I really doubt that.”

Her jaw set, and I thought, Oh, boy, there they go again. Jerome thought so, too. I could tell just by the way he glared at both of them.

“As a matter of fact,” Mom said in her ice-water voice, “I’ve given a lot of thought to taking a full-time job at the country club. I don’t need the high income right now. I’ve got enough saved.”

“I’ll bet,” Dad added.

She stood and faced him. “Clark, I put most of what we saved into an account for the kids. That money’s for them.”

“Isn’t it time for you to take them?” he said.

“Yes,” she snapped at him. “I’m more than ready to leave this house! Where are their bags?”

She was keeping us overnight at the local Ramada Inn. When Dad pointed to the backpacks lined up in the hallway, she turned away.

“Jerome? Hank? Can you—?” Her voice broke. There were little lines beside her eyes that I hadn’t seen before and some on both sides of her mouth. When I turned around and looked at Dad, I noticed he had frown marks in his forehead and something about his whole face seemed to droop a little.

Jerome and I picked up the backpacks, and Sarah went off to the BMW, holding Mom’s hand and her rabbit under her other arm. That rabbit had soaked up about a quart of tears every night. The sorry old thing was probably mildewed by now, but Sarah had him in a stranglehold that Nick Lutazzi couldn’t have gotten out of.

I looked back toward the house before I got in the backseat with Jerome, and I could see Dad through the window, staring out at us and shaking his head. He looked as sad as Mom.

That's when this amazing idea came to me.

They still love each other, I thought. They want to get back together and be a family again, just like we kids want to be a family again. Come to think of it, they probably want it more. Who wants to be in their mid-forties and divorced? At their age, who can they date? What a nightmare.

The first thing Mom wanted to see was how we looked on the tennis court. Jerome pulled a number on her though.

"My arm hurts," he said, rubbing it. "Too much practicing, I guess."

Oh, you guess, do you? I thought. Really put in the time, don't you, jock?

It was a low-down thing to do to Mom, who put injured arms on the top of the natural disaster chart. It never even occurred to her that he would lie about such a thing. She was white faced, running her fingers up and down his arm.

"Where does it hurt, Jerry? It isn't the shoulder, is it?" Her face got even whiter when he pointed to the rotator cuff *and* the elbow. "I'm going to take you to a sports doctor *now*."

"I doubt there is one in Alamar," Jerome said.

"We'll find out," Mom said. She drove us to her motel and we went up to her room and sat on the bed while she thumbed through the yellow pages until she found a listing of all the local osteopaths. Jerome was wrong. There was more than one. There were two.

Both were closed for the weekend.

"You're going to the doctor next week, Jerry," she said, that little muscle working in her jaw that said she wouldn't rest till it was done.

She was massaging his arm again.

"I want you to get X rays. Tell your Dad I'm going to pay for it. Don't even try to talk me out of it. Your arm is no laughing matter."

You're in for it now, Jerome, you nerd, I thought. That'll teach you to comb your hair like some geek.

When we got back to the tennis courts, she concentrated on me since Jerome could only play with his left hand, bum arm and all. It took her all of fifteen seconds to know I hadn't volleyed much since she'd last seen me. Little Sarah did better. She had volleyed off the garage door every day more faithfully than she brushed her teeth.

Mom harassed me and fussed over Jerome and looked sick with worry. The only time she smiled was when she looked at Sarah, who at five years old seemed a shoo-in to be a future star.

"Excellent two-handed backhand, Sarah! Get it in the knees, Hank. You're straight as a stick! When did your feet quit moving? Have you been doing any running at all? Nice lob, Sarah. Remember to hit to Jerome's left; he can't use his right arm. Hank, where's your net game? Come in close, get in my face! Criminy, Hank, I'm almost thirty years older than you, and I'm running you into the pavement!"

"You can say that again," I mumbled.

"What's that?"

"Forget it." I tried a smash and missed the ball altogether.

"It's a disaster," Mom groaned. "A total disaster. Okay, let's try it again. *Come on!* Over the top, Hank! Put some life into it! Great volley off the wall, Sarah! You're looking like a champ!"

A quart of sweat must have rolled off me by the time we quit. Maybe a gallon. I was hobbling and Sarah was skipping.

At this rate, Sarah would be mopping up the court with me in a year or two. Jerome was snickering at me, looking more cheerful than I'd seen him in a month.

I had to do something horrible to him for this. Sneak up on him while he wasn't looking and . . . and do what? In my shape, legs trembling, arms like hot wax, I couldn't even attack a good-sized water bug.

Right then, I felt mad at the world. Mad at

myself because I'd put off practicing until this week and made myself look bad on the court. Mad because I wasn't a "natural" like Jerome. Mad because it mattered so much to me.

Mom put her hand on my head and scratched my wet hair with her short square fingernails, the kind of fingernails any serious woman tennis player has. She smiled at me and the sun streamed down on her, making her hair shine like real gold.

Her face looked full of light, too. The little lines I'd noticed had vanished under the sun. As usual, she had hardly any makeup on and she was blotting off the sweat with her towel, taking even that little bit of makeup off with it, and she still looked good. She also looked happy, even with Jerome's arm lying heavy on her mind. In fact, she looked sort of the way Dad had looked the first night he'd gathered his few cheap gardening tools together and gone out to start working in our weed-infested lawn.

"It'll be okay," she told me. "You'll see. Everything will get better."

She looked hopeful. And strong. Mom was always strong.

"Anybody ready for dinner?" she asked.

Sarah glowed up at her, all her awkwardness with Mom gone and forgotten.

"I am!" she squealed.

Jerome nodded, and I pulled my weary, sweaty bones into the backseat of the car and wondered if I'd live through dinner.

If I'd had any hope that Mom was right and things would look up, it disappeared when the waiter accidentally poured a pitcher of iced tea down Jerome's neck. Usually, he would have just grabbed a handful of napkins and made the best of it, but not tonight.

"You're a total idiot," he said to the boy, who looked worse than I'd felt on the tennis court.

"Jerry, that isn't nice," Mom said. "Apologize, please."

"Apologize?" Jerome said. "Shouldn't he be apologizing to *me*?"

The waiter's lips flapped, but he couldn't get out a word.

"It was an accident," Mom said.

"Like your tearing our lives apart?" Jerome said to her. "That kind of accident?"

"Give us a minute. I'm sorry," Mom said softly to the waiter. She waited until he left to say, "It couldn't be helped."

"It was because you weren't there!"

"We just fell out of love with each other. It's sad, but—"

I jumped up, right there in front of a whole crowded restaurant.

"Stop it!" I yelled. "Otherwise, I'm going to the car."

"Hank," Mom said.

"I just think falling out of love is a pretty lame excuse for breaking up a whole family," I said.

Mom gasped. She put her hand on my arm and looked up at me with tears in her eyes.

"I'm so sorry," she said. "I hope all of you will understand someday."

By now, Sarah was crying, and Mom reached over with a napkin to dry her eyes.

"Come on, baby," she said. She blinked back her own tears and smiled at us. "Hank, sit down. It's okay. I don't get to see the three of you enough to let anything spoil it. Let's have a good dinner. How about it?"

The waiter came back just then with a towel for Jerome and a fresh pitcher of iced tea and mumbled that he was sorry.

"I'm the one who's sorry," Jerome said. "I was a jerk. Though maybe you should let my mom pour the tea this time."

Sarah giggled through her tears, and even the waiter grinned as he handed the pitcher to Mom. I sat back down, trying to remember exactly what Mom had said about her and Dad falling out of love with each other.

Of course, I didn't believe her. They loved each other; I just had to make them remember, that's all. I was thinking so hard that I didn't hear what Mom was asking me the first time and had to ask her to repeat it.

"I asked how you're doing with your schoolwork, Hank. Are you working hard on your algebra?"

"He found a tutor who's a whole lot smarter than he is," Sarah piped up.

"Thanks," I muttered. It's hard to defend yourself when your baby sister is only saying what's true.

4

I'd had only a couple of sessions with Tremont the Terrible, one on Friday afternoon and one on Sunday night, but it seemed like I wasn't quite so dense at algebra as usual on Monday.

I might have been grateful, but every time I looked at Tremont in class I was just full of disgust for him. Out of school, he was turning into my only real pal, but in school he was Mr. Goody Two-shoes.

In the Witch's class, he was just plain obnoxious, writing up her algebra problems for her on the blackboard, running her errands, wearing this dumb expression sort of like *hey-everybody-look-at-me-I'm-the-teacher's-goon.* It was "Yes, Miss Caster, ma'am," every time she so much as looked at him. Before he left the class, he set a sack of his mother's home-dried prunes and figs on her desk. I was going to barf. Just what the Witch needed. A sack of prunes.

I told him on the way home from school: "I would rather flunk than make such a geek of myself."

I expected Tremont to get bitter about my saying this. But he just hung his head and said he knew he was acting like a geek. He'd been doing it a long time and it had sort of gotten to be a habit.

"I guess it's the divorce," he said. Tremont analyzes everything, even his own shame and pain. It didn't seem natural, but my frowning about it didn't slow Tremont down a second.

"I probably have low self-esteem since I never see my dad," he went on in that serious tone of his. "So I try too hard to win other people's respect, especially authority figures like teachers."

Tremont's mother took him to a child shrink for a while after the divorce back when he was nine. That's where he gets his jargon. But when he was explaining it all to me, somehow it rang true. Too true, as a matter of fact.

"By the way, did your mom and dad fight with each other this weekend?" he asked all at once.

When Mom dropped us off at the house yesterday, she'd come inside to talk about Jerome's hurt arm to Dad. At first, they both tried to be polite, but pretty soon they were glaring at each other. They seemed more strangers now than if they'd never met, much less had three kids together.

"Not exactly," I said. Tremont looked like he wondered if I was speaking the truth.

"Anyhow, about Miss Caster," he went on. "I won't write up her problems for her or erase her blackboard tomorrow. It'll be tough, but I'll do it. If she asks me to, I'll say, 'I'm sorry, Miss Caster, but I don't want to erase your blackboard.' "

"Your dumb old blackboard," I said.

"Why do I have to be rude?"

"You've been doing this geek thing for a long time," I said. "You're going to have to do something to break it wide open."

We stopped walking and stared at each other. We'd come to a fork in the road. He had to decide for himself what he was going to do, but no matter what it said about me, I knew that the only way we could be friends was if he made the decision the way I saw it.

A breeze came in from the sea, smelling of salt and seaweed and feeling cool against our sweaty faces.

"Break it open . . .," Tremont muttered.

His eyes shut halfway, the way they do when he's making what he calls "crucial decisions."

Finally he muttered, "Dumb old blackboard."

I drew a deep breath. "That's good. And listen, something else."

He looked at me. "Yeah? I don't know how much else I can do all on the same day. I might go into withdrawal, or I could get the shakes or an asthma attack."

"No, this is something else. It's your name, bud. You can't keep walking around with this 'Tremont' handle of yours. It's going to warp your whole life. From now on, you're just Monty. Okay?"

"What will my mom say?"

"Listen, Monty, are you really going to keep acting this way? *What will my mom say?* You cannot, I repeat *cannot,* go through your entire adolescence as 'Tremont.' You'll end up with a pair of binoculars and a permanent membership in some bird watchers' group. You will never get a date. Hoots will follow you down every hallway." I'd heard some of those hoots already, especially during roll call in the classrooms. I knew he was thinking of it, too. He isn't a dumb guy.

"Monty." He said the name shyly.

"Yeah, it sounds good, buddy. Listen, before we study, you want to skateboard for a while? I've got my board, and Jerome's got an old one you can use."

"Skateboard?" He looked down at his arms and

legs as if he wanted to see them one last time before they got broken.

"I'm not asking you to come down a ramp and jump over four cars. Just a little tame stuff on the sidewalk."

Monty smiled. "I'll give it a try. After that, you owe me an hour in algebra. Not only that, I saw your first history mark. We're adding history to our study period. And handwriting. I'm surprised Mr. Bryant could even read all those wrong answers."

Somehow, I was not all that disappointed. Monty had just made a major breakthrough in his life. The least I could do was let him pull me through the worst part of school. Education.

"You know something, Hank?" he said. "You're kind of a lucky guy."

"Me? How's that?" I thought of Mom and Dad's divorce, not to mention my bad grades.

"Well, I've been noticing how the girls look at you. You know what I heard Whitney Gorman say about you? She told Carol Evans you're so cute you make her crazy."

I could feel myself getting red. "Whitney Gorman, huh? Well, she can find somebody else to make her crazy." Whitney Gorman was sort of cute, I had to admit to myself. But I still didn't really like girls all that much. Not yet. Jerome said he thought I was at least a year away from liking them. He said I was kind of slow, but that he was slow, too. Come to think of it, Jerome had never had a real girlfriend. And he was a senior in high school. Jeez, he must be slower than me.

"Anyhow, you're lucky." Monty sighed. "Do you think any girl will ever say I make her crazy?"

I looked at him and thought, Boy, oh, boy. What do I say now?

Monty said, "Hey, Hank? Don't lie to me, okay? We're at a pivotal point in our friendship. If we start lying to each other now, we'll never be really close friends. Good friends never lie to each other. They may try to say the truth as nicely as possible, but they don't lie."

This wasn't an easy truth. I didn't have any idea how to say it so it wouldn't hurt. But I figured I'd have to. Monty was staring at me so hard with those smart eyes of his that they looked likely to explode.

I sighed. "Listen, Monty, at our age, who's to say what we'll look like when we grow older? But let me say this, buddy. While you're tutoring me, I'm going to start pestering you about what you eat. You really need to take off some weight, bud. I'd like to throw away your peanut butter jar. And your chocolate chip cookies. And when your mom bakes, I'll be glad to eat as much of her baked stuff as possible, just to keep you out of trouble and all. I would be willing to make that sacrifice."

Monty's face was about as red as mine had been when he was telling me about what Whitney Gorman said. But he finally nodded.

"Okay, Hank, it's a deal," he said. "And you can give my bag of marshmallows to Sarah."

What commitment, I thought. I grinned at him and gave him a thumbs-up. "Now I know you're serious," I told him.

Jerome had an appointment with the doctor later that afternoon. Dad took off from work early to go with him. He said he had no idea that Jerome was having all these problems with his arm.

If you ask me, Dad looked a little suspicious. He hadn't seen Jerome with a racket in his hand since we'd moved to Alamar.

He said so to Jerome, and my brother copped out by saying, "Well, you work, right? Wouldn't I practice in the afternoon while you're working?"

"You take care of Sarah in the afternoon."

"Wouldn't Hank help me out and watch Sarah so I could practice?"

Dad just said to get in the car, he was driving him to the doctor. Jerome climbed into the car, holding on to his arm.

What a phony, I thought, wanting to bean my brother.

I was restringing one of my rackets when Dad and Jerome pulled back in the driveway.

"So, is your arm ruined forever?" I asked my brother as he got out of the car. He had a face like a meat-ax.

"What's the matter, jock?" I said. "Bad prognosis?"

"Put a sock in it," he snapped back.

He walked into the house without a second look at me. Dad told me that it was a mysterious thing about Jerome's arm. The doctor couldn't find one thing wrong with it. In fact, when Dad had mentioned that Mom wanted Jerome to play in a country club tournament in April, the doctor said that should be totally all right, if Jerome trained for it during the winter. Sometimes, he said, an arm needed to be used.

When I heard that quote, I was just wishing I'd been there to see Jerome's face.

Anyhow, Dad took out the envelope of forms for us to fill out and send in to Mom's country club for the tournament, and that's when I got the idea. It just came zooming in on me like a jet plane. I'm not trying to say I'm a genius like Monty, but I have my flashes.

Mom had sent all kinds of extra forms to us, in case we messed up. She'd already filled out some of them. Jerome and I were signed up for singles in our age groups and the special brothers' doubles tournament. The brothers' doubles tournament was supposed to be one of those fun specials, so age wasn't important as long as the brothers were between the ages of thirteen and nineteen. Jerome and I would play together like we had last year, when we won second place in the tournament. The Pacific Palisades Country Club tournament was one of the most important on the amateur circuit, and since most of the kids aiming for the pro circuit played in it, second place was not small potatoes. Only Mom and Jerome had been disappointed. Dad and I were giving each other high fives, until we realized we were celebrating alone.

Don't get me wrong. I like to win, too, and first place is way better than second. But Jerome doesn't have to face himself across the net. Maybe it's because I'm used to playing him that I feel like I've done something when I pull out a second place.

And that, Mom has told me, is the biggest difference between Jerome's game and mine.

I told her I thought his hundred-mile-an-hour serve should figure in somewhere, too, but she just threw an arm around my shoulder and said I had no idea how good I was. Yet.

Anyhow, my idea came to me when I noticed that Mom wouldn't be getting the papers back. The envelope was already addressed to the tournament secretary at the country club, where Mom worked part-time as one of the tennis pros. Mom'd be on the road coaching by the time we mailed them in.

That's where the flash came in. I got this really vivid picture of Mom and Dad playing in the couples' doubles tournament, just like they always had. Last year, they'd won it. In fact, they'd won it three times together. Dad is not as great at tennis as Mom, but he's a born doubles player. He's already found a doubles partner at work here in Alamar. They play at least twice a week and hardly ever lose. Mom always said that if Dad had wanted to go on the pro circuit as a doubles player, he'd have had a shot at it.

They'd met on the tennis courts while they were students at UCLA and always looked their best when they were playing tennis together. Laughing, joking. All those things they never did in ordinary life as a married couple. At least, not lately. If they'd just play in that couples' tournament again, it would be like Cupid had shot his full load of arrows into them. We'd all go home together after they won the tournament. Everyone would be happy, and Sarah would stop weeping and wailing and Jerome would stop acting like a nerd and start calling himself "Jerry" again.

In no time at all, I'd made out a form for Mom and Dad for the couples' tournament. Now I just had to hope that the tournament secretary wouldn't mention anything to Mom about it. Who knew, maybe Mom and the secretary didn't even know each other. I also had to hope that Mom wouldn't notice that she got charged extra.

The plan was not without its snags, but it was all I had. I put the form into the envelope with all the others and sealed it before Dad had a chance to check it over. The next morning, it was in the mail.

I'd just used tennis in a way it had never been used before. My brother had always been the star, but from now on, I knew who the real tennis ace was. It was me.

A lot of people say they're going to do things, but Monty really tries to do everything he says he will. That's what makes him amazing.

The very first thing in algebra class, when the

Witch asked him to put the problems on the blackboard like always, he said, "No, thank you, ma'am."

Granted, he was polite as heck when he said it, but it was a beginning.

"Tremont?" the Witch said, watching him. "Did you hear me ask you to put the algebra on the blackboard?"

When he didn't say anything for a long time, I turned around and looked at him. Come on, I thought. Don't stop now, you're halfway home, man.

He looked a little green, but he stuck out his chin and said, "Yes, ma'am, I heard you, but I'm not going to . . ." He cleared his throat. "Uh, I'm not going to . . . to put your . . . your old algebra on the . . . the dumb old blackboard."

I thought I'd bust a gut. Mack Carter swallowed the gum he wasn't supposed to be chewing and had to be pounded on the back by the Witch.

Nick Lutazzi leaned over and punched me on the shoulder. "What's gotten into Tremont?" he hissed.

"Who?" I whispered back.

"Tremont."

"Oh," I said. "You mean Monty. He told me he's sick of the Witch."

Nick's eyebrows went up, but he took a long look at Monty, and there was a little respect in his eyes. Not much, but Monty had years of weirdness to atone for.

I looked around the room and saw everyone grinning. Even Whitney Gorman was smiling. Not that I paid her any special attention or anything, but her hair was sort of pretty, hanging down past her shoulders, looking shiny and golden brown. Her face was nice, too, even though she didn't wear any makeup at all. Only her lips were shiny, like she'd rubbed on that gloss that I happened to notice other girls putting on sometimes.

Suddenly, Monty was on his feet, and Miss Caster was talking to him in that teacher-to-student tone that meant trouble.

She said, "Tremont, I'm gravely disappointed in you."

Monty was still looking pale, but when the Witch said that, he brightened right up. He knew he'd done real good.

"Thank you, ma'am. I mean, I'm sorry, ma'am," he said.

"That's it," the Witch said. "You're getting a demerit. Three pages of extra homework, pages eighty-seven to ninety."

"A demerit," Monty repeated with a glow all over his face.

"This is unusual conduct for you, Tremont. I suspect you've been hanging out with the wrong people lately."

She glared in my direction, looking madder than ever. I couldn't understand what her problem was. Heck, it was obvious. Monty was just saving his own life in the best way he knew how.

After school that afternoon, Monty strolled right into the kitchen with me and helped me make snacks.

"Can I have bologna?" he asked.

"Sorry," I said. "You can have an apple or a yogurt. That's all till dinner." When he looked pathetic, I said, "Every time your stomach growls, just remember this, Monty. No pain, no gain."

His stomach growled. He looked down at it.

"It's funny," he said, "how you can hear something over and over and not really get it until it applies to you. No pain, no gain. I'll take the raspberry yogurt. And a couple of celery sticks."

"And you don't mind that I have the bologna, right?"

"It's only fair," he said. "After all, you don't have years and years of marshmallow and peanut butter sandwiches to atone for."

We took our food with us and went out to work on Monty's forehand, which had improved. Then we worked on his feet, which hadn't. They still looked like they belonged to a gorilla boy.

"I never saw such a huge pair of dogs in my life," I said. "You're the only person in the world who can make tennis shoes look like flip-flops."

"Look at it this way," he said. "If I ever grow into my feet, I'll be about two inches taller than you. Then what will you say, huh?"

"Probably that you're still clumsy as an ox. A tall ox, but an ox all the same. Will you at least try to get up on the balls of your feet? Or have your arches gone totally flat?"

"Not flat," he said. "They roll a little, that's all."

"Rolling arches," I said. "What next?"

We were still hard at it when Jerome came out and said I had to come inside for about half an hour or so. A social worker had made an appointment to see us, and she was here. The final custody papers hadn't been signed yet, and she was making out a report to give the judge.

"Uh-oh," Monty said.

"Nothing to it," I said. But a sickening feeling went all the way down my spine, like somebody had poured something sticky down my insides.

When I saw the woman, I felt even worse. Anna Eisley looked about twenty, and when I sneaked a peek at her ring finger, I could tell she wasn't even married. What did a young woman like her know about how divorce shriveled up kids' insides? Yet she kept on asking us questions and she told us that we should try very hard to answer completely and honestly, that it was all part of the custody proceedings.

"Excuse me," Jerome said quietly. "But how is our private life any business of the court's?"

You could have struck us dead when Anna Eisley laughed. "You know, a lot of kids have asked me that. It's a very good question, but hard to answer." She cleared her throat. "You see, divorce isn't just between two people when they have children. But parents have a hard time seeing past their own pain and their anger toward each other. Sometimes they forget to make sure their kids are surviving okay. That's where I come in. The court asks me to visit you and see how everything's going."

Anna Eisley looked at all three of us, and then went on talking.

"A lot of times," she said, "everything's pretty much okay. You're hurt, but everyone's getting better. When that's the case, I feel like I'm butting into other people's business and that I ought to be ashamed of myself."

Her face got very serious and she stared hard at Jerome, as though only he was old enough to really get what she was going to say next. "But sometimes, despite how it looks, there might be something very much wrong. And if I were to miss that something, like it's been missed many times before, then . . . well, I'd have a very hard time living with that. So I've got to ask my questions and look into your eyes and use all my training and all my intuition to make sure everything is really as okay as it looks like it is. Will you help me?"

She kept her eyes right on Jerome's and didn't smile at all until finally he nodded at her.

"We'll answer your questions," Jerome said for all of us. He looked at Sarah and me, and we both nodded. I didn't like it, but Jerome was our leader. If he said to answer, then we'd cooperate.

Anna Eisley asked us what we did every day when we got home from school and who was home with Sarah and me in the afternoons and did Dad stay home in the evenings or go out a lot. She wrote down that Jerome was with Sarah and me after school, and she asked him how it made him feel that he had to baby-sit every afternoon.

Jerome said sometimes it was a bother, but mostly he didn't care. Besides, I more or less took care of myself, and Sarah was going into a special program after school starting next week, studying dinosaurs. It was called Dinosaurs Galore, and she'd stay at school until Dad picked her up every Tuesday and Thursday afternoon, so that gave Jerome some free time.

"How nice," Anna Eisley said, looking pleased. "And do you like dinosaurs, Sarah?"

Sarah lit up like a sparkler and reeled off the names of at least a dozen prehistoric beasts before Anna Eisley started laughing and held up her hands and begged for mercy.

Then Anna asked us if we needed disciplining often and how Dad went about it. Jerome said that privileges were revoked and that we had to do extra chores around the house. Sometimes, he admitted, we gave Dad a hard time and sometimes he got mad and raised his voice if he was tired or if we were being really horrible. But mainly, he kept his temper and we weren't all that bad most of the time.

"We all try, you know?" he said.

She nodded. "I can see that, Jerome. I really can."

She didn't miss anything that I could think of. She asked us what kind of food we ate and whether

Dad monitored what television shows we watched. She asked us if we brushed our teeth every morning and every night and if we took a shower or bath every single day. I think she was even taking notes about the clothes we were wearing.

Then at the end, she asked us if we had any preference for who we stayed with, Mom or Dad. All three of us just shook our heads even though Sarah would have moved in with Mom tomorrow if she could have. I figured out that she wasn't going to hurt Dad by saying so, and that made me really proud of her.

The social worker smiled at us and said she could tell we really loved both our parents and that they were lucky and we were lucky. She said divorce was not the end of the world.

Sarah said, "How do you know?" She sounded so bitter I couldn't even believe it. I hadn't known Sarah could sound that way. She'd just turned six at the beginning of the week.

Anna Eisley just kept smiling. She said, "I know, believe me. I've been divorced, and I have two kids, and we're all okay now."

I did a double take. She must be older than I'd thought. If I'd known about her divorce before she asked all her questions, I'd have tried harder to give her some better answers.

Well, at least we'd had Jerome for that. He'd covered almost everything in a really honest way that didn't make anybody look bad. He even told about how Mom called almost every night and wrote cards and notes when she was traveling. Presents came in the mail sometimes, too, from the places she flew to with her tennis clients. Plus, she was always asking us if there was something we needed, some problem she might be able to help with.

He told how Mom had wanted to keep Sarah with her, but she wanted Sarah to grow up to be close to her brothers. "Brothers and sisters," Mom had always told us, "should be raised together. You'll have each other long after Dad and I are gone." Jerome told the social worker that, too, and I could see he was happy when she wrote it down.

If she had only known how angry Jerome was at both our parents, she would have been surprised.

"I'll be seeing you," Anna Eisley said. "I'd like you to think of me as your friend now."

When I went back outside, I didn't say anything to Monty for a while, but just grabbed my tennis racket and started slamming balls against the garage door. He sat there watching me.

After I finally stopped, he asked, "Was it disgusting? Talking to that woman?"

I caught my breath while I thought about it.

"It was the same sort of disgusting as watching a cat eat a bug, I guess," I said finally. "It's disgusting, but it's what a cat has to do." Naturally, I was thinking of the social worker as the cat and Jerome and Sarah and me as the poor defenseless bugs.

He nodded. "Oh."

"I'll tell you something," I said. "I wouldn't want her job. Imagine having to talk to sad kids every day who sit there glaring at you like they wished you'd drop dead."

"Yeah. Pretty grim all right."

"One thing though."

"What's that?"

"It made me realize," I said, "that this whole divorce thing is really going to happen. Unless I can find some way to stop it quick."

"*Stop* it?" Monty said. "You mean stop the divorce? Are your mom and dad speaking to each other?"

I thought about the way Mom dropped us off at the house. She honked until she saw Dad at the door, then let us all out of the car. Then as we were going inside, she and Dad half waved at each other.

"Sort of," I said.

"They have to be speaking to each other, or you can't stop the divorce," Monty said.

* * *

I was making some friends at school, even if it took more time with Monty as a best friend. We broke new ground when he had a fistfight right in the Witch's room.

It started with Dwayne Ellis tripping over Monty's big feet just before the bell.

"Watch where you're putting those ugly sneakers, barf feet," Dwayne said on his way to his desk. "Or I'll make you eat your own big fat toes."

Monty's got two weak spots—his feet and his sneakers. Dwayne had nailed them both. In about half a second, Monty rammed him like he was starting tackle for the Pro Bowl. Dwayne's at least two inches taller than Monty and too mean to fool with. He'd just as soon hit below the belt or stick a pencil in your eye.

But Monty caught him off guard, and Dwayne hit the deck.

He found himself on his back with Monty pummeling him with the worst one-two-three jab I ever saw.

Nick Lutazzi said in my ear: "Dwayne doesn't get that he's being pummeled to death by a flea."

"Not yet he doesn't," I said, "but he will. Come on, Nick, do your thing."

"Right."

We just made it. I jerked Monty back and Nick plunked down on Dwayne seconds before his eyes uncrossed.

The Witch came charging over like she'd been in the front ranks all along and took over.

"Tremont, of all people," she said, hauling Monty off to the principal's office.

"Monty!" half the class cheered.

He was wearing a smile as big as a blimp.

Dwayne didn't say anything. He was too busy figuring out a way to live with the disgrace of being on the bottom side of a fight with the class nerd.

He'd just helped Monty change identities. In about ten seconds, he wasn't the class nerd anymore. He was just Monty. All at once, the class loved him.

I guess I was looking better to the other kids, too. My kickball had come back strong, my volleyball and handball were in the next hemisphere compared to the rest of the guys, and I was no longer the last to be picked for any kind of team. In fact, I was usually one of the first. But from what I'd heard from Sue Daniels, the girl who sat in front of me in homeroom, my brother was not doing as well as I was. I didn't see him at school, because my classes were all at the ninth-grade center and he was over on the main campus. But Sue's older sister was in two of Jerome's classes and she'd told Sue that he was the king nerd of the whole class.

"That's weird, your having a brother like that," Sue said, batting her eyelashes at me.

She made me shudder, batting her eyelashes at me while she was running my brother down.

"Jerome," I told her, gritting my teeth, "is not a nerd. In fact, he's a real jock."

"Oh, come on, Hank." Sue giggled.

"He's a little quiet is all. He's just not the kind to talk your ear off, like some people."

The Witch looked our way, and Sue pretended to be reading her science book. "Face it, he's a nerd," she whispered out of the side of her mouth. "If he wasn't, he wouldn't let people call him Jerome."

"Jerome is a great name," I hissed back.

"For what? A new breed of chipmunk?"

Whitney Gorman had heard the whole thing. After we left homeroom to head to our next classes, she caught up with me. "Hank? Don't listen to anything Sue says. She'd find a way to make nuns fight."

"Thanks," I said. "Not that I paid her any attention, you know."

"No, of course not," Whitney said. "I'm sure Jerome is a great brother. I saw him with you at the mall the other day and I thought, Wow, Hank's brother looks really nice."

"Well, thanks again," I said, turning into the science room. Nice, I thought. Brother, you have turned yourself into an all-time loser.

The only thing to be done was to get Jerome playing tennis again, and as quickly as possible. And the only way I could do that was to start playing myself.

Both of us had to train for the spring tournament. And if Jerome wanted to accept any of those tennis scholarships that had been offered to him from colleges all over the country, he'd better start playing. Otherwise, he'd embarrass himself big time and they'd throw him back to the computer department.

5

"I'm not going to take any of the tennis scholarships," my brother said.

"What?"

"I'm going to apply for an academic scholarship," he said.

"Jerome, please. Just saying that is enough to bring tears to Mom's eyes."

He frowned and blinked at me through his horn-rimmed glasses. "I didn't say I wouldn't play tennis in college. Necessarily. I'm just telling you that I'd prefer to go through as an academic, not a stupid jock."

"All jocks are not stupid," I said. "You were an A student back when you were playing tennis, and nobody made a big deal of it."

"Things change." He patted down his creepy hairdo. "Maybe I'm just sick of living my life the way Mom wants me to live it."

"Let me get this straight." I looked my brother in the eye. "Are you giving up tennis because you don't like to play anymore . . . or are you just trying to get even with Mom?"

"I told you I might play in college. *Might,*" he repeated. Not that that answered anything. "Don't take it so hard, little brother."

"Why shouldn't I take it hard?" I yelled in his smug face. "Here I'd give anything to have your talent and you're . . . you're just throwing it all away."

For a second, I saw something in Jerome's eyes that looked like regret. Regret about losing tennis. Regret about the space between him and Mom.

"Didn't I tell Anna Eisley all good stuff about Mom?" he said slowly.

"What you say to Anna Eisley and how you act toward Mom are two different things," I told him.

"Listen, Hank . . . I have a right to see my future in a different way than Mom wants me to see it." He half smiled at me. "Hey, bro. Could we have a change of topic, if you don't mind?"

"Okay." I took a deep breath and came out with it: "How come you've turned into a nerd?"

It was the worst thing one brother could say to another, but it didn't seem to bother Jerome much.

He just shrugged, and then the doorbell rang and he got this stupid look on his face. Even stupider than usual, I mean.

"That's my girlfriend," he said.

"Your *girl*—?"

"That's what I said, wasn't it?"

I couldn't get my mouth to close. After what Sue had told me in school, I never thought it could happen. I followed him to the hall.

Jerome jerked open the door and he and Terri Haggenshaw started going gaga at each other.

No, I thought, closing my eyes for a minute. I can't believe it. This can't be happening.

But it was.

Terri Haggenshaw is a girl nerd. When she pushes her eyeglasses up her nose, she looks like Wonder Woman in her secret identity. If that's not a nerd, then you tell me what is.

I told myself not to panic. After all, this was only Jerome's first girlfriend. It couldn't be serious, not the first one. There'd be a slew of others.

Within a week, I knew it was serious. Jerome was nuts over Terri.

They were together every minute. Instead of doing a nerd solo, Jerome was doing a nerd duet.

Dad said, "Jerry, that girl is very nice. I like her enormously. Intelligent, too."

"Oh, ho, you can say *that* again," I hooted.

Dad ignored me. "What's she going to college to be? A doctor, maybe?"

"A psychiatrist," Jerome said.

"That's handy," I said.

"I think it's wonderful," Dad said. He slapped Jerome on the back and went off whistling.

I'm only surprised he wasn't whistling "Here Comes the Bride." Because marriage didn't seem too far-fetched, the way Jerome and Terri ogled each other through their horn-rims. Had Dad ever thought about the poor *kids* those two were going to produce together? Nerd babies. It was enough to give you the shudders.

"Jerome," I said, "if you ever introduce Terri to Mom, Mom's going to gross out."

"I don't think so." Jerome smiled dreamily.

"You can tell just by looking at her she's never had a tennis racket in her hand," I warned.

"That's the best thing about her," Jerome said.

"Jerome, she's kind of . . . I mean, nobody says she has to be on the cover of a magazine or anything, but . . ."

"But what? I love the way she looks. Little brother, I like everything about her. Absolutely everything." He squinted at me. "What's the matter? You got some problem with Terri? She's nuts about you."

"No," I said. "No, I think she's great. Honest. It's just . . ."

"Just *what?*"

"Nothing. She's great. Terrific." And a girl nerd. With horn-rims and flat hair.

But Terri had never done anything to me except not be pretty enough to be my brother's girl. In fact, she sometimes brought me gifts, things she bought with the money she made baby-sitting. Like she heard me say how much I like Lamborghinis, and one afternoon she showed up with a Lamborghini model car kit with paint and glue and everything. I wasn't going to bother making it, but Monty had a fit wanting to help me, and it turned out awesome.

That's when Monty got high on Terri. He even said, "Maybe it's only the ugly girls who are cool. I think maybe I'm going to marry an ugly girl when I grow up."

"Monty, for Pete's sake, talk sense," I said. "I'm not saying that people should just pick out good-looking people to marry and that the rest doesn't matter. But it's a *little* important how your girlfriend looks, isn't it?"

"I guess." He frowned. "You know what? I don't like that word 'ugly.' I'm sorry I even used it. The real truth is that *nobody's* ugly, Hank." He bright-ened up. "You ever think how often we change our minds about how people look? Back when Nick Lutazzi was making fun of me all the time, his face looked like his butt to me. These days, with him smiling and joking with me, he doesn't look half bad. And the longer I know Terri, the better looking she seems."

"Well—"

"Take me. Admit it, you think I'm better looking now than when you first met me, don't you?"

"I'm not looking to date you, buddy-o." I glanced at his waistline. "Besides, you really *are* looking better now that you're laying off the peanut butter. You're not a macho man yet, bud, but you're improving."

"So, maybe Terri will improve, too. Just like me. Give her a chance at least. Okay?"

"Well, sure. I'll do that."

It sure is complex. Life, I mean. Here I was with a best friend with an overhead lob for a serve, a brother with a girlfriend from genius camp, and no dog to my name, no matter how many times I asked Dad for a puppy. But Monty was right about Terri. She deserved a chance.

"The thing about you," Monty told me, "is you think every girl's supposed to look like those babes in bikinis on prime time. Don't you get it, Hank? You're a victim of programming."

"Whatever," I said. There was a babe on my favorite TV show who was just about right for my brother. She looked about as much like Terri as a hot fudge sundae looks like a bowl of cottage cheese.

Oh, well, I thought, Terri was only Jerome's first girlfriend. You had to practice somewhere. He'd probably pick out a totally different kind of girl to marry.

For that matter, why bother to marry anybody? It was going to end up in divorce, anyhow.

Dog came to live with us at the beginning of October. When we first moved to Alamar, I had asked Dad for a sheepdog and he said maybe. A sheepdog, a big fuzzy sheepdog. I could see him in my mind. His name was going to be Sinclair. I liked that name.

Dad showed up after work one Wednesday with a puppy for a surprise. He was only a few weeks old and Sarah said he was the cutest thing she ever saw and she was in love with him, but he'd better not eat her parakeet.

But he wasn't a sheep puppy. He was a dumb peek-a-poo. That's a cross between a Pekingese and a poodle. He'd always be a fluffy little dog, even when he grew up, Dad said, like that was a terrific plus. He'd never get too big for our house. Another plus was that he was free. Dad got him from his friend at work whose daughter's dog just had a litter.

Dad took him out of his jacket and handed him to me, and then he said, "Oh, no, that dog just did his business all down my shirt. It's pouring outside, too, so I'm wet from the inside out."

I handed Dog right back and said, "No, thank you. I don't want him."

Sarah right away said, "I'll take him."

Dad looked real sad standing there with Dog in his hand and rainwater dripping off his hair. When I pushed Dog away, it was like I was pushing Dad away, too. But somehow, I couldn't keep myself from pushing.

Dad couldn't figure out what to do. At first, he almost handed Dog to Sarah. Then he said, "No, Sarah, you got your parakeet; this dog belongs to Hank. Come on, Hank, you can at least give this little guy a try. He's wet and shaking all over. If you'll hold him, I'll go out to the car and get his food."

Jerome and Terri came in. Terri said Dog was the most adorable thing she'd ever seen and I almost said, "If you like him so much, you can have him." Dog was trying to get into my shirt, so I unbuttoned it and he crawled in and stopped shaking.

The idiot dog had adopted me.

Dad slammed back in through the front door, carrying a soggy bag full of dog food. Rain dripped from his clothes and ran down his glasses. He said,

"Hank, I'm wrong. If you don't want this puppy, it's not fair to make you keep him. You deserve a dog you can love."

Dog's damp fuzzy body snuggled up inside my shirt. His breath was warm on my chest. It would have been a really neat feeling, if only he'd been a sheep puppy.

"Hank, I could take him and—"

"No," I said, sticking out my jaw. "It's not fair to walk away from somebody just because you don't love them."

Dad stared down at me. Jerome and Terri were staring at me, too.

To heck with them. To heck with all of them.

I went to my room and shut my door. Dog and I lay down on my bed.

He let out a long, contented dog sigh and cuddled up closer, and in just a few minutes he was sound asleep. Probably he was dreaming he was a sheepdog, but the poor thing was never going to get close to *that* dream.

Darn Dad anyhow. He not only had to get me an idiot peek-a-poo, he also had to get one that fell in love with me at first sight.

When you're stuck, you're stuck.

For two weeks after that, I kept after Jerome, trying to get him to practice tennis with me. I reminded him we'd want to look good for the brothers' doubles, and besides, he needed the practice for his singles match.

"All things considered," I told him, "you want to be at your best for the tournament."

"Bro, I don't quite know how to say this . . ."

"What?" I didn't like the smug look on his face.

"Hank, I've decided not to play in the tournament. In fact, I wouldn't play in the tournament if an eight-hundred-pound sumo wrestler were sitting on my Adam's apple, telling me to cry uncle."

The blood drained right out of my head. I almost had to sit down.

"Not play in the tournament?" I mumbled.

The big goon smiled. One of those triumphant

smiles that makes you want to kick it off a person's face.

"What about going pro, Jerome? What about all those dreams you had?"

"Don't go hysterical on me, little brother. There are more important things in life."

"Like becoming a couch potato?"

"You're one to talk," he snarled at me. "But I'm not playing in that tournament and I'm not going to be a pro tennis player, no matter what Mom says."

"Like it was just her dream."

"It was."

"It was yours, too, guy. You talked about it all the time."

"Well, I'm not talking about it now!"

The two of us glared at each other until it suddenly occurred to me that I wasn't helping matters any.

I made myself sort of smile at him and said, "Jerome, I'm sorry. I really am. It's just that I was thinking it would be good for our mental health if we played in this tennis tournament."

"My mental health is superb," he said. "I don't need a tennis match to prove myself."

He was grinning a little. Jerome is the type that can never stay mad. It seemed a perfect time to take advantage of his good nature. I couldn't tell him my plan about us playing in the tournament so I could get Mom and Dad to play in the couples match together. I'm not dumb enough to tell my brother something like that.

But I understood how to get to Jerome. I ducked my head, trying to look confused and under the weather.

"Well," I said, "maybe *I* need to play in this tournament, Jerome. I think it would help me to, you know, work out some stuff."

My success was so quick, it almost made me feel guilty.

"Oh," he said. My big brother looked like he'd accidentally squashed a ladybug. Jerome might be tough on the court, but off the court, he has a soft heart.

He said quietly, "Sorry, Hank. I was only thinking of myself. Sure, I'll play brothers' doubles, if you want to do that."

The next week when our mother called from Arizona, she was thrilled. She said she'd heard from the tournament secretary that our forms were in and signed.

"Isn't this going to be fun?" she said.

"Oh, yeah," I said. "It'll be great. By the way, did the secretary say anything else?"

"What do you mean?"

"I meant about if the forms were filled out okay."

"Everything's fine," she said.

"Great," I said. "I'm really looking forward to playing and all."

Jerome looked at me a little suspiciously. I hadn't told him I'd already filled out the forms. And forged his signature while I was at it. Lucky for me that the second we both hung up our extensions, the phone rang again. It was Terri for Jerome and by the time he got off the line, Dog and I were lying across my bed, pretending we were asleep.

I lay there thinking: Either Mom and Dad are going to fall back in love with each other . . . or they're going to kill me.

"They're going to kill you," Monty said. "But the punishment might start even before they find out what you've done, Hank, if you know what I mean."

I knew what he meant. He was staring down at my report card.

It was October sixteenth, the end of the first term. I'd done all right in the subjects Monty had been tutoring me in, a lot better than I'd expected, in fact. The Witch gave me a B in algebra, and I actually scraped out an A in world history from Mr. Bryant. It was everything else that was a disaster.

Monty had never even *seen* a report card like mine. Neither had I, actually.

"D in English." Monty sounded awed. "D minus in life management skills. How'd you screw that one up?"

"It was my money management project. You have to plan your first apartment and furnish it and leave yourself money to live on."

"So what kind of furniture did you buy?"

"A coffee table. Oh, and a really great projector TV set and a black leather couch. What else would I need?"

He shook his head. "Chorus, C minus. That's supposed to be a freebie. Explain to me how the heck you get a C minus in music."

"Maybe she could tell I wasn't opening my mouth when we sang?" I wondered why I'd even opted to take chorus instead of a study hall. Talk about dumb. But there was once a time when I liked to sing and Mom had always told me I had a good voice. Since the divorce I didn't like to sing worth doodley. C minus. Served me right.

"D plus in earth science."

"Mean old Mrs. Kurtz is almost as bad as the Witch," I muttered. As if putting a plus beside it made a D look any better.

"And I warned you about the handwriting. You refused to let me help you." He stared at the handwriting column that ran alongside each subject. "Wait a minute. This is in algebra, not English or history. You mean the *Witch* gave you a C minus in handwriting? In *algebra*?"

"She says she can't read my equations," I said.

To make it worse, every teacher except Mr. Bryant had asked for a parent-teacher conference. Miss Caster had written: "I am suspicious of Hank's quick improvement and will be monitoring his behavior."

"She's accusing me of cheating," I said. "All that hard work to be called a cheat. I hate her."

"We'd take her to the principal if your other marks were good," Monty said. "As it is, the principal might believe her, not us."

I sighed. "I'm dead meat," I told him. "Outside of algebra and history, the only thing I got good marks in is citizenship."

"That's better than me," Monty said. He whipped out his own report card and folded it to the citizenship column before I could get more than a peek at what looked to be straight A's.

There before my eyes were grades to compete with my own. First Miss Caster's grade. Of course, his fistfight and his rudeness had practically guaranteed the Witch's D. Then Mrs. Kurtz's grade: C minus. (Monty had refused to do the earth science project with Dwayne Ellis after their fight, no matter if Mrs. Kurtz had assigned them together or not. Now Monty and I were doing it, which might help my next science grade.) I looked on down the page. With every teacher, it was the same. Monty had surpassed himself. All C's and D's. And the same note worded differently: "Tremont's behavior has changed alarmingly this semester. A parent-teacher conference is requested."

I said, "Man, oh, man, if we put our two cards together, we'd have a dunce and a juvenile delinquent."

Monty studied his report card for a while longer, then suddenly turned to me and stuck out his hand. "Thanks," he said, as we shook. "Maybe I'll ease up a little next term. I was just making a point."

I glanced back at my card and said, "Thanks for the A and the B. It's the only thing keeping me from being thrown to the sharks."

"We'll do better next time," Monty said. "But you're going to need a full-time tutor. I'll take you on, buddy."

Surprisingly, I felt a huge wave of relief. "Thanks, guy."

He grinned mischievously. "I've got a great idea.

Let's improve everything else to A's and B's, and bring your handwriting down to a solid F. It'll drive Miss Caster Oil nuts."

"Why should we want to do that?" I asked.

"Because," Monty said, "she's your homeroom teacher and hands out the report cards. She must have seen you were in trouble academically this term. She's a real jerk for making a bad situation even worse."

There's something about the way Monty understands life that makes me think it wouldn't be so bad to be an honors student. He even said he'd like to go with me to show the report card to Dad. That way, he could point out the A in history and the B in algebra, and explain that from now on, he'd be tutoring me in every subject.

"I'm thinking your dad will be okay about it then," he said.

Monty turned out to be right. Mainly because he talked Dad's ear off before he even let him see the report card. By then, Dad knew not only what he was getting ready to see, but what Monty promised him he'd see next term. I got away with just a short lecture. The punishment, Dad said, could wait until next grading period. Since Monty was so sure of himself, and since he'd already delivered on two subjects, Dad said we deserved a chance, especially with the move and "everything else that had been going on." He went back to his lawn, where a few patches of grass were actually starting to sprout here and there, amazing the entire neighborhood. Dad was learning the art of fertilization.

Monty and I took Dog out to the backyard and the three of us just sat there on the grass, panting.

"No punishment," I said. "Nada. Zilch. Thanks, Monty. You want me to go with you to see your mom about your grades in citizenship?"

Monty grinned. "I don't think we'll let her know you helped me there, buddy. Not if we want to keep hanging out together."

No doubt about it. My best friend's got a lot of style.

By the time Mom got back to Alamar, it had been almost a month since we'd last seen her. She'd been on the road, coaching one of the up-and-comers, a sixteen-year-old girl who was already ranked in the top twenty on the circuit. Mom thought that within a year, Carmen might be a major contender in the Grand Slam tournaments.

None of the three of us could have cared less if Carmen had just won Wimbledon. That's how hurt and angry we felt toward Mom for disappearing for so long. When she pulled the car into the parking lot next to the public tennis courts and opened the car door, none of us moved.

"Come on!" she said. "Let's hit the courts."

"I don't want to," Sarah said clearly.

"Me either," I agreed.

"No wonder you wanted us with Dad," Jerome said. "Lucky for you that you could unload us."

"I guess," Mom said, sounding aggravated, "you're just never going to understand."

"Understand *what?*" Jerome snapped back at her. "That you show up here once a month like clockwork no matter how much of a nuisance it is?"

"What could I do about it, Jerry?"

Before Jerome could say a word, I said, "Well, for openers, you might try cutting it back, Mom. It's like you've laid out your life so that you're with us one percent of the time and on tour the rest. I guess your tennis clients must feel real important to you, but to be honest . . . your kids *don't*!"

She turned so white that for a minute I thought she might pass out, and then she just slammed her car door and started driving again, up one street and down another. Finally, she parked in front of an ice-cream shop, and we didn't even want ice cream.

Our visit went downhill from there. That night at the motel we all sat on the beds and watched TV sit-coms without anyone cracking a smile. I tried to laugh once, and it came out like a bullfrog's croak. Jerome shot me a look. I gave up.

By the time Mom took us home the next day and was standing outside the house hugging us good-bye, she was crying and it didn't help that the only one who hugged her back was Sarah.

"I'll do better," she said, looking at each one of us in turn. "I promise you that I'll do better."

"You mean, after you get back from Australia in three weeks?" I asked.

She gave a kind of gasp, then said, "Yes. Then."

I stood with Sarah on the sidewalk, waving while Mom drove off, but Jerome just turned his back and walked into the house.

7

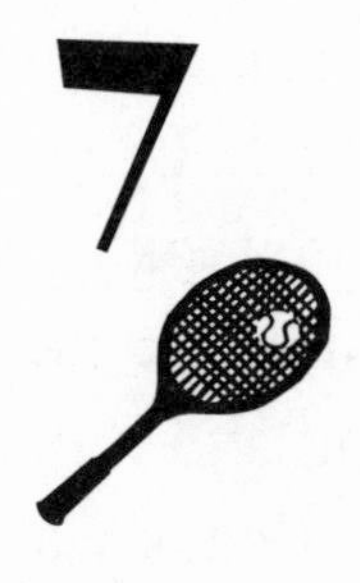

By November, I knew we were in trouble. If Jerome and I were going to play in the brothers' doubles and the singles matches that he didn't even know I'd signed us both up for, we were going to have to start playing tennis. Jerome humored me a little by volleying against the garage door and told me not to worry. We'd play well enough by April. We'd do a little practicing later next year.

"Next *year*?" I said. "You mean, you're going all through Christmas and the New Year without picking up a tennis racket? And we're supposed to win?"

"Who said we were going to win?" Jerome said. "Winning is not important, little brother."

"It isn't?"

"Sports," he said, "are for fun."

"It's going to be fun getting our faces rubbed into the pavement?"

"Won't bother me," he said.

I remembered his sulking over our second-place showing last year and wondered where that Jerome had gone. All this Jerome wanted to do was hang around with Terri and study and eat.

So here's what I did. I started pestering him all the time about it. Everywhere. Around the house. After school on the campus.

"Time's going by, Jerome. Come on."

"Not today, Hank."

"November sixth, Jerome."

"I can read a calendar."

"November seventh and counting, Jerome."

"Keep it up and you'll be counting without your front teeth, Hank. I said lay off!"

"Ah, looks like November eighth to me, Jerome."

By the middle of November, he sure did hate my face.

"It says something for him that he really hasn't taken out your front teeth yet," Monty said admiringly. "Listening to you carp at him, I feel like socking you myself sometimes."

"Believe me, I haven't even begun to carp at him, Monty."

* * *

I even followed Terri and him to the Burger Shop on a Tuesday afternoon while Sarah was taking her Dinosaurs Galore class. I sat across from them in their booth and made Jerome spring for a milkshake while I bugged him about playing tennis with me. If I were as obnoxious as possible, maybe he'd play a little to get rid of me the rest of the time. There were only so many times he could say no.

"No," Jerome said, for at least the fortieth time. "No way. Wrongo. Zilch. Strike out."

"I don't understand." I let the corners of my mouth droop downwards. "You said you'd play brothers' doubles with me."

"I will," he said calmly, slurping his shake. He was starting to put on a few pounds. If nothing else, playing tennis might keep him from becoming el blimpo. Bad enough to be a thin nerd. A fat one is the bottom of the barrel.

"What are we going to do then?" I put my elbows on the table and glared at him. "Play like a couple of barfs?"

Terri giggled. Jerome slurped again.

"Are you really that enraged at Mom that you want to go out there and humiliate yourself in front of everyone?" I asked, and Terri giggled again.

"Enraged," she repeated, like that was a screamer.

"It's stupid to think you can humiliate anybody over a game of tennis," Jerome said.

"But tennis is what you *do,* Jerome."

"I want a life in science, not some stupid sport," he said.

"Why can't you have both? You won't be a tennis pro for much longer than age thirty, for Pete's sake."

"You have to make a choice," he said.

"I don't get it. *Why?*"

He didn't answer. He'd finished his shake and now he was cramming his burger down his throat. He didn't even take the onion out, and Jerome hates raw onions. He says they make his throat swell up and leave a taste in his mouth like a hamster slept in there.

It was awful to look at him swallowing that burger whole, so I looked at Terri instead. Compared to Jerome, she looked terrific. At least she didn't have tomatoes and onions hanging out of both sides of her mouth.

"Did you know Jerome is awesome at tennis?" I asked her.

"I didn't know he played any kind of sports," she said. Something about the way she said it, kind of shy yet hopeful, told me she was liking the idea that her boyfriend had a hidden streak of jock in him.

"If he wanted to," I said, "Jerome could be another Pete Sampras."

Her mouth dropped open.

"He's that good?" she asked.

Jerome looked at me like he wished my side of the booth would drop into a hole. A hole maybe as deep as the Grand Canyon.

"Is he that *good*?" I whistled. "Jerome could make millions at tennis. The way endorsements are today, he could make a hundred million, no problem. He could be famous. Oh, well. I guess it's worth more than being a millionaire to get back at Mom. Even though he could be sacrificing his future and his wife's and kids' futures."

"Oh, baloney," Jerome mumbled through his last bite of burger.

"Be nice, Jerome." Terri pushed up her glasses with her finger. She had a line between her thick eyebrows. She was thinking harder than I'd ever seen her think before, and girl nerds go pretty deep.

Jerome mopped french fries in ketchup and wolfed them down by the handful.

I leaned over toward Terri and whispered, but he could hear me as well as she could: "He's just furious at Mom for traveling so much. That's why he won't even pick up a tennis racket. He'll end up being so rusty that there's no way he'll be able to play in the brothers' doubles with me, even though that will just about kill me." I gave it my best shot to look eaten up with misery and desolation.

"Finish your shake and get lost," Jerome said.

Terri leaned toward me. I was all ready to hear her say "a *hundred million*?" She'd fallen right into my trap, no doubt about it.

She whispered: "Hank, tell me the truth. Was tennis really that important to Jerome?"

I set my glass down and grinned at her. I suddenly found myself liking her. A lot. Then I spied Monty walking Dog not far from one of the Burger Shop's two front windows and got up.

"I guess I'll see you later," I said, then leaned over and whispered in Terri's ear: "It was the most important thing in the world to him. And it is to me, too. I really want to play in that tournament with him."

Jerome glared at us. "Didn't anybody ever tell either of you that it's rude to whisper in front of somebody? I mean, I am in the room, in case either of you missed it."

Terri sent him a smile, but she didn't apologize. She just said, "When is this tournament?"

"The first of April. That just leaves us a little over four months to practice. I know it sounds like a lot, but it really isn't. Everyone else has been practicing like crazy all year. Believe me, Terri, we're rusty as heck."

"I see." She nodded a little.

I left quick. When you're finally making progress, you don't want to wiggle your own ladder.

"Well?" Monty said as we started toward home. Dog was pulling hard on his lead.

"Jerome's not easy, Monty. Terri's with us, I think, but I'm still going to have to take some sort of action. I can't believe my brother is doing this number. He thinks he has to make a choice between being a scientist and a tennis player. Did you see him? He's getting fat, for criminy's sake. I'm going to have to get that weight off him."

"If anybody can do it, you can." Monty glanced down at his own body that was looking better every day. "You know Rusty Carson who sits in front of me in homeroom? The heavy kid who never says much? He was asking me how I lost all the weight, and now he wants to lose some, too. So I told him I'd check with you and we'd put together some menus for him."

I groaned. "I'm turning into a flipping nutritionist. Okay, we'll help Rusty. But about Jerome. It isn't only the weight, Monty. The weight would probably take care of itself if I could get him back on a tennis court. I know that if I could just get him to play one game, he'd be hooked again and he'd be back to playing every day. You never saw him play. It's like he comes alive out there. Believe me, he loves it."

"No kidding." Monty thought about that for a while. "So what are we going to do?"

"Take drastic measures, Monty."

"Drastic measures," he repeated.

I shrugged. "Nothing else is working."

Two days later was Thursday, Sarah's dinosaur class again, so after school, Monty went to the main campus with me to find Jerome before he had a chance to leave school. I was carrying a couple of cans of tennis balls and his favorite racket, the one I grabbed out of the driveway the night he quit playing tennis. I'd restrung it myself and it was ready for action. All I really needed was Jerome.

Monty spotted him heading toward the parking lot and his dilapidated old car, slouching along, carrying Terri's books. He looked like a couch potato in need of a couch.

"He's really as good as you say?" Monty asked.

"Believe it or not, he's terrific," I said, hoping he still was.

The minute Terri saw me with the tennis racket,

she smiled at me and took her books back from Jerome and his, too.

Jerome stopped walking and frowned at me, but I didn't let that stand in my way. I just kept going until I was right in my brother's face, tennis racket and all.

"Hey!" I said brightly. "Great day for a volley, huh?"

"Not today," Jerome said, frowning harder.

"Please. I've got my own racket in my backpack and a couple of spares."

"You're bothering me, Hank. Get lost."

Terri stepped in. She smiled at Jerome so hard that her braces shone in the sun.

"Jerome," she said, his name sounding like melting honey in her mouth, "you are going to play tennis today."

He smiled back at her weakly.

"No, I'm not," he said.

"Yes, you are," Terri said, and leaned over and kissed him on the cheek.

Actually, Terri was not so bad-looking. Not at all. Once she got those braces off her teeth and maybe got some new glasses that weren't so dark and horn-rimmed, or maybe even some contact lenses, she might be kind of pretty. Even if she didn't do any of that, I was starting to like how she looked. It was just like Monty had said. I wasn't seeing her glasses anymore; I was just seeing Terri. And man, oh, man, I was glad to have her on my side.

Jerome looked at me, then back at Terri. His eyes slid toward his tennis racket. I was swatting at the grass with it like it was a golf club.

"You're killing my racket," he said with a groan.

There's always that moment when you really know you've got somebody. When Jerome said that, I knew I had him.

He jerked the racket out of my hand and said that if I was in such a hurry to get slaughtered, we should grab a court and get on with it.

"Let's go!" I jogged ahead of him before he could change his mind. This was no time to give Jerome a chance at a getaway.

We nabbed the last court, just ahead of two of Jerome's classmates. He had once pointed them out to me. He said they thought they were cool dudes. The tall blond kid was Brian. The taller, blonder kid was Dustin.

Jerome stripped off his sweater, and I unloaded my backpack on the bench next to Monty, who kept watching Brian and Dustin while I got out my racket.

"They're not giving up." He frowned at me.

I turned around to give them an eyeful of what a

tennis ace looks like. Nobody was going to stop Jerome from playing tennis that day. These two incredible jerks weren't going to interfere with my plan.

"They'll give up all right," I said.

But Brian and Dustin just kept coming. They totally ignored Jerome, like he wasn't even worth a look-see, and concentrated on me.

"Hey, kid," Brian jeered at me. "You're on the main campus. No babies allowed over here."

"Yeah," Dustin agreed. "We'll take this court, if you don't mind."

Jerome was stretching out by the baseline, facing the sun. Since he didn't say anything, I had to go lay it on the line for him.

"Jerry," I said, using his jock name for the first time since we'd moved to Alamar and he'd gotten tough on the "Jerome" handle. "Are we really going to allow those jerks, who look about as bland as two vanilla milkshakes, to bully us out of this court?"

Jerome picked up his racket and swung it.

"Hmmm," he said. Then he glanced over at Terri, who was fidgeting on the bench. She had this letdown look, like her macho guy had just turned back into the wimp she knew and loved.

"Jerry?" I asked.

"I don't know," Jerome said.

I got a sudden inspiration. It was a beaut.

"Hey, dudes," I said, grinding out a smile for Brian and Dustin. "What would you say to our playing you for the court?"

For a minute, they couldn't even react they were so stunned. Then they bent double and laughed themselves to the pavement. They couldn't even breathe, that's how tickled they got at the idea of playing the nerd and his baby brother. Tears actually rolled down their cheeks.

"I love it," Dustin said.

"Okay by me," Brian said.

Dustin pulled out his racket. "Best two out of three," he said, still chuckling. "Then the losers have to let Brian and me—that is, the losers have to let the winners—have the court."

"Deal." I grabbed my racket.

Jerome shot me a glance. He didn't look mad at me anymore. In fact, he looked like he was about ready to laugh, too, but he didn't. He just cleared his throat and said we should all volley a bit, and then Brian could serve, if he wanted.

Terri was off the bench now, standing on the sidelines. She was chewing on her thumb like it was a steak dinner. She probably had never seen a nerd beat a jock at his own game and didn't even know it was possible to do it. I waved at her to try to cheer her up.

"Come on, Terri," Monty said. "Sit next to me. We'll be the rooting section."

She managed a faint smile. "All right."

She more collapsed than sat next to Monty, and he patted her on the shoulder. They were joined in misery.

"Okay," Jerome said, "let's volley."

Brian served the first ball to Jerome, and he hit it into the net.

"Oops," Jerome said. "Hit it to me again. I bet I can get it over next time."

Brian hit a slow one to him, and Jerome went to hit it back and missed it completely. For a horrible second, I thought maybe Jerome was so out of practice he couldn't even hit a baby shot over the net. It scared me so much the blood left my head.

"Double oops," Jerome said, and winked at me.

My heart stopped hammering, and I could breathe again.

Gotcha, I thought, nodding at my brother. Then, so as not to be outdone by Jerome, I hit a couple into the net.

By now a few high school kids had gathered by the court.

"Hey, everybody, come on over here!" rose up in the air. There was a sort of thrill to the atmosphere.

Some girl said, “I can’t look,” but I didn’t notice her going anywhere.

We went on like this a few minutes longer, with the Cool Dude twins showing off for the crowd and Jerome and me tripping all over ourselves, and then Brian said it was time to play our game. He and Dustin were tired of fooling with us. The sooner they played two games and won the court, the sooner they could get their exercise.

“You can even serve first,” Brian told Jerome.

Dustin said, “Yeah, if you know how to serve.”

The crowd giggled.

“You want me to serve? Jeez, I’ll try,” Jerome said, and carried a couple of balls back of the service line. “Let’s see . . . I think . . . yeah, you just sort of throw it up over your head and smash it down, right? I think I’m starting to . . . yep, by golly, it’s starting to come back to me. Ready, bro?” he asked me.

“Ready, bro.” I grinned back.

He threw a ball two yards into the air and came down on it with his racket like a pound of TNT colliding with a lit match. The ball zoomed in on Brian at a hundred miles an hour.

Brian yelped and jumped back.

“Ace!” I cried. “Jeez, big brother, that really was an ace if I ever saw one. You got lucky.”

"Yeah," Dustin jeered. "Although anybody worth his salt could have put it back to you." Brian still looked white enough to pass out. I had often stood on the other side of Jerome's serves, and it wasn't a pretty position to be in.

Even more kids began to gather. It was turning out to be an event.

"Hit me one," Dustin bragged to Jerome, "and I'll show you how fast I'll cram it down your throat."

"Don't get me nervous now." Jerome winked at me. He was really getting into this.

His next serve, this one shooting up off the line on a sharp bounce toward a tender spot of Dustin's anatomy, made his first look like something served up by a Cub Scout.

A squeak came out of Dustin, and he got a roar from the crowd.

By now, the tennis players on the other courts had stopped playing their games and had joined the crowd watching ours. Terri looked so lovesick staring at Jerome that anybody could see how she felt. That is, if anybody except me had been looking at her. Everyone's eyes were on Jerome. He was awesome. I hadn't been putting Terri on when I told her my brother could be worth millions on the pro circuit. Hadn't our mother told us so many times?

Out here, playing against a couple of high school duffers, he looked like a tennis god come down from the sky.

Not that I was so bad myself. With Jerome on my side of the net, confidence flooded into my veins like new blood being pumped in. Me and my brother, we could beat any ten players put together.

In that first game, I never hit back one ball because neither Brian nor Dustin could even come close to returning one of Jerome's serves. I had to wait for Brian to take over service to see a ball come over to our side of the net.

The first ball came to me, and I almost made Dustin eat it. Another inch and he would have had a tennis ball for a mouth.

"Yeah!" Monty yelled from the sidelines, and gave me a real macho arm pump. "Lookin' *good!* Lookin' *real good,* bud!"

Terri was clapping so hard her hands must have hurt.

In fact, all the high schoolers were solidly lined up for Jerome and me by this time. The more they yukked it up, laughing at how Jerome and I were killing the Cool Dude twins, the more the Cool Dude twins didn't have enough sense to quit. They seemed to think the whole thing was some hideous accident. They kept trying to beat us, even after we'd finished the two-out-of-three test.

I whispered to Jerome, "Good thing for them we're out of practice."

"You can say that again. These guys are pitiful."

But they just wouldn't give up.

"Make it four out of seven," Dustin begged.

"Fine," Jerome said.

Then they wanted to play a whole match. Here is the incredible thing. All this time, they had not volleyed one ball back over the net to us. Not one ball. Their only points came from me—two double faults on my serve and a couple of botched returns on their serves. Heck, I knew I was rusty.

Jerome called me over.

"Okay," he said in a low voice. "Let them play a little. I want to get a volley going."

"You're calling the game, bro."

We eased off and extended their misery. After all, we had to practice for the brothers' doubles. These chumps were better than nobody to volley with. But it was funny how quick the old killer instinct kicked in to me. It was almost impossible not to brain them with a fastball every other return.

By the second set, Jerome and I really started to get our old brothers' doubles synch going. We could almost read each other's thoughts on a court when we had "The Synch" between us, and it felt good to have it again. Mom used to get tears in her eyes when she'd watch us play together.

While Dustin and Brian yelled at each other and collided at the net and the baseline, I covered the long shots while Jerome took his game to the net and smashed balls into the other court like he was throwing over live hand grenades.

He was on fire. He had come back to his own destiny. Everybody knows it when a person just sort of falls into his life's true plan.

And everybody knew it that day.

The crowd had grown humongous, and they were all applauding us. The girls ogled Jerome. He sure looked like Macho Man out there. I noticed Julie Marie Reineker was there. She was a girl Jerome used to mention and stare at a lot when we first moved to Alamar. But up till now, she hadn't given him the time of day.

Julie Marie sure looked good, even if she had the heart of a witch. She was wearing a white fluffy sweater and combing her long blond hair with her fingers, and she watched Jerome like a starving dieter eyeing a slice of chocolate cake. No wonder though. When Jerome's got a racket in his hand, there's not an ounce of nerd in him. If Julie Marie was practically crawling over the concrete toward him, she wasn't alone. There was a lot of panting going on among the girls right then.

Just as I started to worry about what all this ogling would mean for Terri, I saw Jerome looking toward the sidelines. He didn't see any other girls there but Terri, not even Julie Marie. He just kept smiling at Terri like a guy in love, and she kept smiling at him like a girl in love.

And we kept slaughtering Dustin and Brian.

Finally, they had the sense to quit. Their faces were red as tomato juice. I could understand why. I mean, it's bad enough to lose at all when you're these kinds of stuck-on-yourself guys. But it must be horrible to lose to somebody you've been calling every geek and nerd name in the book. They dragged themselves off the court with all their so-called friends sniggering at them.

After that, just Jerome and I played, and nobody else played on the other courts. They just hung around our court and watched us pound balls to each other. I think Jerome and I felt pretty much the same way. Like how great it was to do something you were really good at. About how not doing it is a waste.

I wondered if I felt even better about it than Jerome. Because Jerome really is a brain, and he can do a lot of things, even play classical guitar and read philosophy and learn languages. He gets a thrill when a chemistry experiment goes right. But though Monty might turn me into a decent student one of these days, I'm no brain. I'm not a musician and I don't like to read anything, much less philosophy. The only science experiment that ever turned out right for me was the one I did with Monty. But that day, I really got how great it is to excel at something.

I knew one thing for sure. I was never going to give up tennis again, even if the divorce did go through.

By late November, it was obvious what my dad's favorite part of the evening was. He'd settle down with his paper in the den and wait for Monty's after-dinner tutoring session with me to start. After-dinner torture session would be more like it.

And Dad loved it.

Probably because Monty grilled me worse than Dad had ever hoped or dreamed. Next to Monty, the Witch was a trip to Disney World. Sometimes, when we were right in the thick of it, Dad's paper would start shaking, and I could tell he was laughing his head off back there. Having a heck of a time.

"If you chart your life like you just charted that tide, Hank, you'll be in dangerous waters most of the time, let me tell you!"

"Anything's got to be better than this, pal."

"Oh, yeah! In case you've forgotten, report cards are coming out next month and you'll be looking at big-time exams."

"It's weeks away, already."

"Have you forgotten how much those midterms count?"

"I remember, I remember. You're killing me, Monty. You're taking out my brain and stomping on it something awful. I'm surprised I can get it back into my head after one of these sessions."

"Tides and the ocean floor."

"Bore, did you say?"

"Shut up and start drawing. And make sure I can tell what everything is. Last night's chart looked like all oysters on the half shell."

"At least it was in the right family. Shows I'm trying."

The day after midterms started, something weird happened. When my English teacher handed back my literature test, I saw I got two wrong. Monty had worked with me for three solid nights, filling my head so full of Stevenson and Maupassant and O. Henry that I had dreamed my brain exploded. I woke up with my hands around both ears. It was a horrible experience.

"Two wrong!" Monty groaned. "How could you miss two?"

"Out of fifty," I told him, showing him a solid A paper. I couldn't help grinning. I'd been doing better in most of my other subjects lately, but English and science were still hard nuts to crack. I'd been getting C's on every test in both subjects. "It's the first A Mrs. Gordon gave me all year. We ought to celebrate by taking the night off."

"Celebrate?" Monty grabbed the paper. "We've gotta crack down on those books. You've got history and science midterms tomorrow. You know you and science."

But he smiled as he smoothed out the paper. He didn't give it back. The next time I went to his room, I saw it hung on his bulletin board in a place of honor. There are times when Monty is actually close to being a sentimental sap.

It started raining in early December. People who don't live in California have no idea how hard it can rain out here when it tries. It went on for days and nights. We sprung at least four new major leaks in our house, especially in the living room and in the master bedroom. But the rain really hit its peak one night when Monty and I were doing algebra. That storm was a real cloud buster. Buckets of rain, along with loud booming thunder, and some truly mean lightning.

"Awesome," I said.

"Crippling," Dad said, getting another pot. A new leak was starting in the living room. We had pots and pans from one end to the other.

When the knock on the front door sounded, at first we thought it was part of the thunder and nobody answered. But the knocking just went on and on.

Dog's barking clued us in, and Sarah was the first to run to the door. When she opened it, Monty's mother was standing there holding a plate of homemade candy and carrying an umbrella as big as a tent. Laura Singer's a nice woman and pretty, always smiling at me and trying to get me to eat when I'm at their house. One of the first times I ever really talked to her, she said, "So *you're* the one who threw my peanut butter away. Tremont's lost ten pounds so far, and I've lost about five. Thanks, Hank."

The only things I really had against her were the name "Tremont" and those cheap sneakers she made Monty wear. She just had no idea how demoralizing it was for a kid to walk around in generic brand shoes. I mentioned it to Mom, since she gets shoes on discount because of the pros she trains, and she said I could give Monty a pair of great shoes for Christmas. I'm hoping Monty's mom gets the message without getting mad or anything.

I'll say this for her. Even in the middle of a rainstorm, she brought good vibes in the door with her. Not to speak of the homemade candy.

"I came to get my son," Laura Singer said, laughing as she lowered the umbrella and stepped into the hall. "Unless he wants to swim for it."

Monty looked up with his mouth open. "I'm not ready yet. There's an algebra test tomorrow—a new section. The way dumb head takes to it, I'm liable to have to sleep over."

"Well . . ." Laura stared at the one umbrella she'd brought. The rain poured harder and lightning crashed so hard she jumped. There was something very lonesome about her as she turned to look out the window. It was so black and threatening out there.

Sarah grabbed the candy plate. "Buckeyes!" she shrilled. "And caramels and chocolate creams. Mmmmm!" She stuffed her mouth so full, she couldn't get her lips together.

Dad was already in the hallway, taking the umbrella and ushering Monty's mom inside while he brushed the rain off her coat. Along the way, he took the plate of candy out of Sarah's greedy little paws.

"Chew what you've got there, Cookie Monster, and then we'll see," he said. He patted her hair and went on talking to Laura Singer about the storm and all the leaks we'd just found out about. She gave him the name of a local roofer and said she'd call later and give him the number, and then both of them wondered about local flooding and said they were glad we were on high ground that provided excellent drainage.

"That new housing project, you know the one—?" Laura began.

"Pinecrest subdivision," Dad said with a nod. "A real mess."

"It's completely flooded," Laura said. "And I happen to know the people in that subdivision all paid top dollar for their homes. A friend of mine bought there and she's sick. Just sick."

"The land in Pinecrest isn't sound," Dad said. "One of my clients, an engineer, worked on that project and he predicted the first big rain would take them out."

"He *predicted* it?" Laura said. "You're kidding. You'd think there'd be a law to protect—"

"Wouldn't you?" Dad agreed. "But you know how these things work. And now the home owners will all have to file lawsuits against the builder, and with the big money being where it is, I'm not sure—"

"I know just what you mean," Laura said. "Horrible. Corruption everywhere. But people's homes are one area that should be protected. Proper drainage should be a right, not a privilege."

Growing up seems to provide fascination about building lots and drainage and community services and taxation. Dad and Laura were wrapped up in it, and by the time Jerome drove up after leaving Terri's house, they'd already moved into the kitchen and made fresh coffee.

"Will you concentrate, knot head?" Monty asked. I think I might have inspired a future teacher. If he lays into his students the way he does me, somebody'll throw a notebook at his head.

Jerome wandered into the den and sat in Dad's chair with a dreamy smile on his face. The way he kept touching his mouth, I knew for sure he'd been kissing Terri.

I was relieved he still felt that way about her. After we beat the Cool Dude twins, I'd been sure that sooner or later, she'd be chopped meat. Girls had been calling the house for Jerome one right after the other, but he wouldn't give any of them half a chance. One of these days though, I'd kept thinking, temptation would just get to be too much for him.

But looking at him that night, all at once I knew for sure he was sticking to Terri. I hope when I'm a high school senior, I'll see through glasses and braces and recognize a girl who's worth getting that dreamy kind of look over.

I hope there's another Terri out there. All of a sudden, I thought of Whitney Gorman. She'd been smiling at me a lot lately and saying, "Hey, Hank, how's it going?" whenever she saw me, and lately, I'd started saying, "Hey, Whitney," right back at her, sometimes even before she spoke to me. I smiled like an idiot just thinking about her. My smile probably looked like the goofy smirk Jerome was wearing.

"Hey, oaf brain. Will you concentrate? Or are you going to break all records for stupidity tomorrow? Huh?"

I sighed and faced Monty's scowl. "Okay, okay. By the way, Monty, what sort of job am I going to have where I figure out algebraic equations? My dad's a friggin' *accountant* and I've never seen him trying to figure out how A over C equals Q."

"You're getting sarcastic again, Hank."

"I just want to know the use of all this stuff."

"The way life works . . .," Monty began, getting his guru's face in place.

"Yeah?" Despite my best intentions, I'd begun to be interested in Monty's theories on how life worked.

"Certain requirements simply *are,*" Monty said. "It was all worked out in another sphere. Somewhere, so long ago that it's beyond time, it was decided that the human brain couldn't develop right unless it could figure out equations. We don't want your brain to turn into a legume, do we, Hank?"

I sighed. "Does a legume brain function okay on the tennis court, Monty?"

"Nope," he said. "Not at all. There's a lot of malfunctioning legumes out there—you see them on the tennis court, you meet them in everyday life. Believe me, Hank, you don't want to be one of them."

You have to give up eventually, when you're dealing with Monty. He can outlast you every time.

I got up and ran around the room, screaming, "Oh, help me, pleeeease! My brain's turning into a lima bean. *Eeeeiiiiii!*"

Monty was right after me, tackling me like he was the athlete and I was the nerd. We wrestled around for a while, and even though Monty was much thinner now and more athletic than he had ever been in his life, I knew I could have twisted him into a pretzel without much problem. But what the heck, I let him win. I didn't really want to have a bean for a brain.

"Let's get down to it, Hank."

"Where's your mom?"

Monty sent a smiling glance toward the kitchen. "I'm not worried about her. She'll stick around for a while."

Then we really got serious with equations.

Somehow, we had started to settle down. Every day, I was thinking more about the possibilities of being a tennis pro. Hadn't Mom put a tennis racket in my hand as soon as I could stand up? Weren't half the people on the circuit related to other people on the circuit? Most tennis pros come from tennis families. And we were all back on the court and playing good tennis.

Dad was building a good list of clients at his job, and his grass was starting to come in. The only thing was, it was mostly crabgrass. By now, neighbors were gathering around our yard every weekend afternoon to give Dad advice. How to weed, how to fertilize, how to prune trees.

Sarah was probably the most improved of all of

us. She wasn't crying much anymore. Any time anything went wrong or she got really lonesome for Mom, she knew to call her right away on her portable. She and her rabbit would cuddle up on her bed with the telephone and pretty soon, you'd hear her giggle.

"Oh, yeah?" she'd say. "You wore sneakers and a long black skirt? And *pearls*? Oh, jeez, Mom."

Once she listened for a minute, then started laughing so hard she could hardly breathe. I asked her what Mom had said.

Sarah looked up at me from her pillows. "She said, 'Feet are everything.' "

I had to sit down on Sarah's bed and laugh along.

Other stuff was improving, too. Jerome had a nice girlfriend and was playing tennis. Scholarship offers were pouring in. I was doing better at school, thanks to Monty, and my newest report card proved it. Only one C in earth science, with the rest B's and A's. Monty was mortified by the C, and said he was thinking about making a tape that could play in my ear while I was sleeping.

"That way," he said, "you'll be cramming your brain full of science all night long."

"Yeah," I said. "And I'll be reciting it all the way to the loony bin. Forget it. No tape."

"It's that or really knuckling under, pal."

“So I’ll knuckle under,” I said, wondering how much more studying a brain could stand.

Just after midterms, Mom called us from Mexico City, and a week later she flew home and drove straight to Alamar. She had two weeks of Christmas vacation and moved into a motel on the beach that she’d found on one of her long walks along the ocean. She fell in love with its Olympic-sized swimming pool and Jacuzzi, its clam and oyster bar, and its private stretch of clean sandy beach. Since she was going to be spending a lot of time in Alamar, she said, this place would suit her very well. She could have taken us to her great condo in Pacific Palisades, because she has all holidays with us, but that didn’t seem like a good idea to her.

Not at Christmas.

Christmas should be all family, she told us. Anyhow, Alamar was growing on her. I could tell. I could almost see her wanting to move in with us.

“Oh, yeah, Alamar. It’s great,” I said. “Smell the sea air. We love living in a seaside town, you know. Even when we don’t see the ocean, we can smell it in the air and feel it in the good old salty breezes.”

She grinned at me. “Hank, you sound like an Alamar brochure.”

“Sure. It’s great, Mom. Wonderful.”

All of a sudden, she got serious. “I’m so glad you’re happy. You’ll never know how I’ve worried about that.”

“Don’t talk dumb,” I said. No kid likes to hear that kind of thing. And no kid likes to see tears in his mother’s eyes.

“Those are happy tears,” Sarah said. She couldn’t quit smiling, what with having Mom in town for two whole weeks. She’d crawl into Mom’s lap and play with her necklace and love anything that came out of Mom’s mouth. I’ve heard that we depend on the same-sex parent to let us know what we’re supposed to be like when we grow up. If Sarah grows up to be like Mom, she’ll be thin and beautiful and full of energy. She’ll also be kind and loving and a great tennis player.

“It’s a shame,” Jerome said to Mom, “how much Sarah misses you. Don’t you feel guilty when you see how much she clings to you when you’re around? Don’t you realize how unhappy she is when you’re not?”

“Please don’t, Jerry.” Mom put her hands around Sarah’s ears as if she couldn’t bear for her to hear what Jerome had just said. “Don’t you know how much I love you three? Don’t you think I’m trying to find a way to have more time with you?”

“Are you *really*?”

"Yes," she said. "I really am."

Jerome looked at her for a long time. Finally, he shrugged. "Okay. Truce. Let's go to the courts."

"Are you sure that's what you want to do? I thought you might rather get a picnic and take it to the beach."

"Nah," I said. "We'll head for the courts. Let him pummel me to my knees. It'll make him feel great."

That brought a little laugh from both Mom and Jerome, which is what I'd been after. Hank, the peacemaker, had saved the day again.

If I wanted to keep the family together, I had to make everyone get along. And the best way to do that was to get everybody to the courts.

We were a tennis family. We all did better when we were playing the game. Of course, Jerome really did wipe up the court with me. But for the first time ever, I managed to win an actual set that day.

Must be an accident, I thought. Maybe Jerome's sick today. It can't be me.

Somehow, I'd connected with a lot more balls than usual. Maybe I was just having a good day.

"You weren't bad out there, bro." Jerome grinned at me. "In fact, you were fairly terrific."

It was the biggest compliment my brother had ever given me.

I felt like I needed a string to tie me to the earth.

By February, we were in top form again. Jerome and I played every day, and Sarah volleyed with the garage and with Monty, who by now owned a good racket and had taken up the sport with his usual zest for everything that life could offer. Dog had become an expert at fetching stray tennis balls. Dad was playing more tennis, too, with his doubles partner from the office. He was in training and didn't even know it.

We were organized and ready for the tournament.

And the brothers' doubles were staring us in the face. Also the singles tournaments that I'd signed Jerome and me up for.

The one I didn't like to think about much was the couples' doubles that I'd signed up Mom and Dad for.

I kept waiting for it all to hit the fan. I'd even jump when the phone rang. I'd think, This is it. Mom's found out. The jig's up.

But there had only been silence. Months of it.

"Maybe," I said to Monty, "it's all going to work out just like I planned."

He didn't answer for a minute. Then he took off his glasses and cleaned them, and said, "This coming summer I'm getting contact lenses. Though maybe I don't need them anymore. I'm getting pretty popular now. Have you noticed?"

We'd been working with Monty's feet for the last hour. It was like the last remains of his old nerd self had settled in those dogs of his, and I wondered if we'd ever get them out. But aside from his feet, he looked good. He was suntanned and twenty pounds lighter than when I first met him. His shorts fastened in the right place.

"Yeah, I noticed," I told him. "You're also much better looking."

"You sure it's not just you getting used to me?"

"I've noticed a couple of girls looking at you. Including Marcy Webster."

He blushed. "Marcy just wanted help with algebra."

"Marcy's an A student. She could teach algebra."

He smiled. "I like that about her. I like smart girls."

"Me, too," I admitted. Whitney was a good student, too. Lately, she'd sometimes call me to compare class notes in history, which we took together, and a couple of times we'd even eaten together. Well, not exactly together. At the same table in the school lunchroom. Neither Monty nor I could say we had girlfriends. Not yet, anyhow. Maybe by our sophomore year, I thought. We might start off by double-dating together. That way, we could talk to each other if we couldn't think of anything interesting to say to the girls. All in all, dating was one of the scariest concepts I'd ever tried to take in.

But right now, it wasn't an issue. We had left the driveway and were alone under the big oak tree by Monty's back porch, staring over the comfortable clutter of what had somehow in our minds become one big yard instead of two.

Monty said, "Feel that, Hank. The winds of California February are blowing over the land. Betcha next month will seem like spring."

"Winds of California February," I muttered. I still had to shake my head at some of the stuff that came out of his mouth. Even more surprising was that I'd started to enjoy hearing it.

Monty put his glasses back on and suddenly stuck out his hand to me for a shake, like he has a habit of doing when he's reached what he calls a significant moment in his life.

"Thanks, Hank," he said with that serious look of his. "You know, buddy, I owe you a lot."

I thought of my decent report card that had just come out. Straight A's, if you didn't look at music. I still couldn't sing worth beans. Why is a baritone voice so much harder to control than a soprano? But the rest was all A's. I had become a student.

I shook Monty's hand. "I guess I owe you, too, man."

He kept looking at me.

"Hank . . . about this couples tournament," he said. His smile faded.

"Yeah?"

He cleared his throat. "You remember how I once told you that good friends never lie to each other?"

I nodded.

"Well, Hank, there's more than one way of lying. One way is to lie outright. But another way is to just keep still about something and never tell your friend what's really on your mind. And, well . . ."

His voice died away. He was having real trouble speaking his mind today. Usually, he wouldn't have hesitated to stand up in the United Nations and tell the leaders of the world how they were really screwing up world peace.

"What's the matter?" I asked.

"Well, Hank, this couples' doubles thing has been bugging me lately."

"And?"

"It's just that with your mom and dad not knowing about it and all . . . well, it's not going to work, Hank. At least, I don't think so. I wouldn't be your friend if I didn't tell it to you like it is." He looked worried. Like he thought our whole friendship would go down the tubes. Maybe that was why he'd shaken my hand.

I took my time to think about exactly how I should answer him.

"Monty, I understand that you've got a superior brain to mine," I finally told him. "And I also think that you've got some sort of power that the rest of us don't have. You seem to know stuff. So if you say it isn't going to work, I take that to heart. I really do. But when you want something as much as I want this, you have to try for it, even if you end up making a real turkey of yourself."

He sighed deeply and shrugged. "You thought about how you're going to get them on the court? What'll you do, just hope they're both in the stands when their names are called for their match? Then what? I mean, you really think they're gonna walk out there and play tennis together?"

He pushed his glasses up higher on his nose and waited.

I looked up into the pale blue sky, with its drifty clouds. "I don't know, Monty. Probably you're right and when they hear their names called, they'll jump up and start yelling at each other right there in front of everybody. How does this sound? Maybe I'll tell them what I did when we go to L.A. next month for the tournament. Wait a minute, I know. I'll tell them just before their names are announced, so they won't have time to think about it. I'll just try to make it fun. If I'm lucky, they'll be good sports and go along with it."

"And if you're not lucky," Monty said, "you'll be wearing your head as an ankle bracelet."

I looked at him. "Just because I let you get away with your doom-and-gloom predictions, guy, doesn't mean you can keep pounding away."

He grinned. "Or what?"

"Or you'll be wearing *your* head below your belt. Believe me, a few poor citizenship marks and the loss of twenty pounds don't make you a champion in the ring. I've still got more force in my pinkie than you've got in your hands and your feet put together, and we both know it. Don't test me, buddy."

He nodded. "But what I was wondering, Hank."

"Yeah?"

"You think I could drive down with you? If nothing else, it could make a good chapter in my book."

He has this book that he claims will someday be a best-seller. He writes it every day and has never offered to let me read it. Once when I asked, he said, "I'll let you see it if you want, but it's no big deal, you know, Hank. It's just our life. Stuff I share with you every time we talk. When my book comes out, you'll be in it."

As we sat there side by side in an afternoon that would have been empty without each other, I said, "So, you really want to go to L.A. to see this rotten egg explosion you're predicting?"

"It may not be *all* rotten egg," Monty said. "More like an egg roll than a rotten egg. Full of surprises. And if it all goes bad for you, well, I'd like to be there for you, anyhow. At least, maybe everyone's less likely to kill one another if there's a witness to see the gore."

I took my eyes off the sky and looked at Monty. There have been times I've admitted to myself that I know him better than I've ever known anyone.

"I'll ask," I said.

He smiled. "Thanks, buddy."

Here is what I told Dog: Life never seems to get to a spot where you can say I've finally got it together, or all the old problems are gone, at least. It only gets to that point, I guess, when you're dead. Which is probably the biggest difference between life and death.

Dog sighed, as if he totally understood what I meant. He was in terrible trouble himself, having failed to learn both the importance of being housebroken and the taboos on table-and-chair teething. If he'd owned a doghouse, he'd have been living in it, but luckily he didn't, so he wasn't.

Actually, if he'd owned one, I'd probably be living in it with him. Because yesterday afternoon, it all hit the fan for me.

It was the second week of March, and Sarah and Jerome and I were all dressed and ready to go with Mom when her car pulled up outside. Dad looked toward the window, put his paper down, and started to walk us toward the door, when all at once it happened.

Mom's car door exploded out toward the street and she came out of it like she'd been shot from a cannon. You only had to look at her face to say, "Uh-oh."

I knew what was going to happen, and yet I couldn't think of a way to react. My brain seemed to be running on dud batteries.

"She's coming in," Dad muttered. He outweighed Mom by about forty pounds, but he looked scared.

Jerome didn't look too hot either. We hadn't had one of these rip-roaring family free-for-alls in a long time, and none of us looked forward to them. To put it mildly.

Only Sarah looked hopeful. "Maybe she's changed her mind about wanting the divorce," she said. "Maybe she's fallen back in love with Dad."

"Look at her eyebrows," I said. "Are those the eyebrows of a woman in love?"

"She's found out," I muttered, picking up Dog, who had caught my anxiety and had just made a new stain on the rug.

Jerome heard me. His eyes were on me, sharp as switchblades. "What do you know about all this? You'd better tell me quick."

But there was no time to tell anybody anything. Dad opened the front door and Mom busted through it. Before your heart could beat, the whole ugly business was out in the open, with Mom screaming she wasn't going to play in any couples' doubles with a man she was divorcing, and how tacky could Dad be to have thought of such a thing? Then Dad was yelling even louder that he *hadn't* thought of such a thing, and how stupid did she think he was, anyhow?

Then when they had both yelled their best, they stopped all of a sudden. They'd both remembered at the same time who did the signing up in the first place.

They both turned to me.

"Hank?" my mother said.

Dad didn't say anything. He didn't even look like he could breathe.

Then everybody, even Sarah and Jerome, was looking at me and I couldn't think of what the heck to say. That idea about the couples' doubles had seemed so bright, and now it looked weird and crazy. *I* looked weird and crazy. I held Dog closer to my chest, and he looked up at me and licked my chin. Dog was the only one I wanted near me. The rest of my family looked like strangers, all at once.

"Why did you do it, Hank?" Dad asked quietly. When I just shook my head and kept staring at Dog, Dad knelt down in front of me and looked up at me so I'd have to see him.

"Hank." He stared right into my eyes. "Here's the way it is, son. It won't work. Your mom and I wouldn't be a couple again, even if we played in the couples' doubles. That's something we all have to accept. It's one of those tough things that just *is*. I wish I could change it for you, Hank. But I can't. Neither can your mom. I know, because for a long time, we both tried. And we couldn't. Do you understand, son?"

I said nothing several times over.

"Anyhow," Dad went on, "the divorce is . . . final, Hank. It went through several days ago."

"Oh," I said. "I just thought that . . . well, everything would be perfect now if . . . if Mom could only come home. That's all we need now to be happy. That's *all*."

As soon as I said it, I knew I'd just asked for the one thing that Mom and Dad couldn't give me. I could ask for a trip to the moon and they'd try to get it for me. But I couldn't ask Mom to come home.

She had her hands over her eyes now. Her shoulders shook and she was actually sobbing out loud. Dad kept wiping his glasses and clearing his throat, and Jerome had tears in his eyes. Sarah had hold of Mom's skirt and was crying hardest of all.

If Dog hadn't whimpered, I'd never have known I was squeezing him so tight. I whispered, "I'm sorry."

Dad said, "That's okay. I think I understand. I think we all understand."

Jerome cleared his throat. "Yeah, Hank."

It was funny how they all thought I was apologizing to Mom and Dad. *Really,* I told Dog in that silent language we used to talk to each other, *I was apologizing to you for squeezing you too tight.*

I carried him to my room and shut the door behind us. I wouldn't even open it when Mom came after a long time and knocked on it and asked me to go with her and Sarah and Jerome. I told her to go on without me. She kept on pleading with me to let her in, but I wouldn't, and finally, she said, "Hank? I love you."

Not long after that, I heard the front door close and the quiet thump of car doors slamming shut.

Then the only thing I heard was creaking floorboards. Dad was doing his pacing. He hadn't done any pacing since we'd left Los Angeles and come to Alamar. This pacing was all my fault, pure and simple.

Oh, well.

Like I told Dog, there's no running away from your sack of troubles. He had to learn not to chew up the furniture and make stains on the rug, and I had to learn that my family was never going to be the same ever again. And the second I'd seen Mom get out of her car, I'd known what Monty was trying to tell me that day, the thing he couldn't say right out. "Don't break your heart wishing for things that can't be, Hank. Life is already tough enough."

But it got even tougher. I could hardly drag myself to school the next Monday. Whitney said, "Hank, are you running a fever? You look terrible!"

You'd expect that when a girl tells you you look terrible, she'd look grossed out, but Whitney touched her hand against my forehead for a second and sort of smiled before she took it away. Then she said, "Well, it's not the flu anyhow. What's the matter, Hank?"

I leaned against my locker, not very far from where she was putting books into hers, and said, "Family junk." I was surprised at myself for saying such a personal thing, because I'd never said anything more personal than "Go stuff yourself" to a girl who had once stuck her tongue out at me. And that was back in third grade.

Whitney closed her locker and said, "Family. That's the worst."

"You have something happening in your family?"

"Everybody has stuff happening in their families," Whitney said. "Mine's different from yours, but it's still bad." She got a funny look on her face. "I've never told anybody this except for you, Hank. My dad's been sick. He's real overweight and he had a heart attack and almost died. The worst thing is that once he got a little better, he started smoking and eating wrong again right away. My mom got furious. I mean so mad she can hardly speak to him right now. She says she feels like he's betraying the whole family." Whitney sighed.

"Middle-aged people are idiots, aren't they?" I said.

"Sometimes I think none of us is very smart," she said, and smiled at me. "At least not all the time. Now tell me what's happening with your family, Hank. Or don't you want to say?"

I didn't, but after what she'd just told me, how could I say no? So I told her the whole thing, aiming my words at my locker. I got red just telling her my big idea and how stupid it had turned out.

Now, I thought, she'll look at me like I'm the biggest loser she ever saw.

She didn't. She smiled at me again. "A pretty good idea, really."

"They didn't think so."

"*I* think so," she said. She changed the subject before I could crawl through the vents in my locker and disappear. Boy, that girl could probably talk to presidents and not make a fool out of herself. "That's neat about your playing in the tournament with your brother. You mean like doubles or something?"

"Yeah. Brothers' doubles," I said.

"You're playing with Jerome?" somebody said in back of me, and I turned to see Nick Lutazzi. "I wish I could play tennis like you," he said. "I've never known anybody who could play like your brother and you."

"Me neither," Mack Carter said, popping his gum on his way to English class. "Somebody told me your brother is going to be worth a zillion dollars. Will he buy you a BMW?"

I wished I could tell him I wanted to be a pro, too, but I couldn't say it out loud. It didn't even have anything to do with BMWs or making money. I just flat out wanted to play tennis. Hadn't I spent most of my life so far getting good at it? Wasn't it in my blood?

But it was more than that. My family was happiest on the courts. It was when we were playing tennis or watching the Grand Slam tournaments on television together with pizza and soda, all of us yelling at the set and laughing and getting excited about some play, that we'd seemed the most like a whole family. Now we weren't whole anymore, but when I faced Jerome across the net or played as his doubles partner, I could still feel it. That great feeling of family.

By now, we were all on the move, because we had a matter of seconds to get to class. I got to science just as the bell blasted. A thundering sound like a herd of elephants on a stampede told me Nick Lutazzi hadn't made it and had started to run. By some miracle, the roof didn't come down.

I took a seat and told myself I was feeling a whole lot better now, but there was still a dull achy feeling inside me. Part of the time it was in my heart, and sometimes it was jammed square between my shoulder blades.

One way or the other, I was hurting.

It didn't wear off the way most hurts do.

And all at once, I was too tired to play tennis. Now the shoe was on the other foot. Once I'd used to whine to Jerome about practicing. Now he was whining to me. Although he was a lot more abusive than your average whiner. He said, "Hey, droop face. First of all, get that look off your mug. Then knock off the moping around and get your sorry butt back on the court with me."

I tried, but I couldn't put any heart in it. The way I limped around the court, I could have used a cane. Then I started falling asleep in classes. I was a wreck.

Monty told me he understood and put up with me. He said with my long face and bad attitude I was no joy to be around, but he would be my friend through the bad stuff as well as the good. But he started bringing a book to the backyard as a defense against my worst moods, when I wouldn't volley or talk and would just sit there staring into space. Sometimes he'd leave me sitting there and go walk Dog, who was feeling as put out as anybody else.

I was no fun to be around. Not for anybody.

And the tennis tournament was getting closer and closer.

Pretty soon, it was April.

A week before we were supposed to leave for L.A., I got called to the principal's office. When I got there, Monty was sitting in the front office, looking as nervous as I felt.

"Your part of the last science project," Monty growled at me as I dropped into the seat beside him. "You wrote it yourself, didn't you?"

"What do you mean by that?" I shot back.

"You didn't copy it out of a book or anything?"

"Would I do something like that, especially when paired with the king of ethics? Anyhow, I wouldn't do it, even if I were failing. Plagiarism's disgusting. Even if my English teacher says that Shakespeare did it on a regular basis."

"That's a danged cop-out, saying that Shakespeare did it."

"I told you I didn't do it, Monty," I said through my teeth. "Shakespeare is the plagiarist, not me."

"I didn't think you would," he muttered. "It's just that you haven't been yourself lately. Who knew how low this whole thing might have brought you?"

"It didn't bring me *that* darned low," I said.

"I'm sorry, Hank. I just can't figure out why we're sitting here."

"I don't get it either. I've been too drained of energy to get into any real trouble, even if I'd wanted to."

The principal's office door opened just then.

"Come in, boys," Mrs. Shane said, and smiled at us as she followed us through the door and shut it behind us.

Monty and I gave each other relieved looks. If she was smiling at us, it couldn't be too bad. We took seats in front of her desk and waited. My heart sounded like my own marching band.

Mrs. Shane pressed the intercom button that connected to her secretary's desk. "Harriet, would you buzz Miss Caster to come down, please?"

"Miss Caster?" I blurted out. You weren't supposed to speak until you were spoken to when you were in the principal's office. But there was something about Mrs. Shane with her black hair and shiny rose red lips and friendly smile that almost made you forget you were in trouble.

Monty looked puzzled. "What does Miss Caster—?" he began.

"Let's wait until she gets here," Mrs. Shane said. She looked at me. "Hank, I haven't talked to you since you got settled into Southwest High, but my attention was called to the great improvement in your report cards. You got the Most Improved certificate on award day, didn't you? Congratulations."

I pushed my thumb at Monty. "I had sort of a tutor."

She smiled. "That's terrific." Her eyes lingered on Monty as though she was surprised and pleased at what she saw.

Monty said, "Does whatever we've done have something to do with Miss Caster, ma'am?" It was like him to stick to his point.

She just smiled and waited until finally there was a light tap on her door. A moment later, Miss Caster walked in the room. She sat down, too, wearing the kind of smug expression that you might expect from a teacher who had once given a kid a C minus in handwriting . . . in algebra no less.

"I'll let your teacher tell you what this is all about," Mrs. Shane said, leaning back in her chair.

Miss Caster cleared her throat. "It's about your absences this term," she said in her uptight voice. "Both of you are past your limit."

There was dead silence in the room. Monty's jaw dropped open. I couldn't believe what she had just said.

Monty answered her. "Hank and I were both out of school for over a week with the flu," he said. He was just barely holding his temper. His old Goody Two-shoes days were long gone. Monty didn't have one polite note in his voice. "You called us into the principal's office to complain that we were sick?"

Miss Caster stared at him. "I couldn't fail to notice that the two of you got this 'sickness' of yours at the exact same time."

"We hang out together a lot," Monty snapped, "so one of us caught it from the other. But we both had doctor's excuses. Dr. Bennett, the same for both of us. Call him now, if you don't believe me. That way, you'll know we didn't have a chance to ask him to lie for us, since you've got a low opinion of our honesty. He's in the phone book, on Marilla Avenue."

A little blush crawled down Miss Caster's cheeks.

"Shall I get the phone book?" Mrs. Shane asked. She opened her bottom drawer, but Miss Caster shook her head.

"I'm not challenging you on your doctor's excuse, Tremont," she sniffed.

"Monty," he said, sticking his chin out at her. In a minute, the two of them would be duking it out.

"I'm not saying that it's a foregone conclusion that you didn't have the flu, I'm just saying the timing was suspicious." Seeing that Monty was about to have at her again, she hurried on. "Actually, I'm much more worried about this tennis tournament you're planning to attend next week."

"You know about that?" I said.

"I assume that everyone knows about it," Miss Caster said. "In case you haven't read it, this morning's edition of the school newspaper is devoted to how you two plan to take off from classes and go to Los Angeles to play tennis. Quite an example for the other students, isn't it?"

“We won’t be missing that many classes,” I said. “The second week of the tournament is during spring break.”

“I’m sorry, Hank,” she said. “But it’s not appropriate to take off from school to go to sporting events. Especially when you’re both already past the allotted number of absences. Illness is one thing. But for a sports event, I’ll be forced to penalize you both one letter grade for every day you’re illegally absent.”

Even my brain could figure that one out. One letter grade a day at three days. That would bring an A to a D. It would bring a B to an F.

“You’re not for real,” Monty said slowly.

“I assure you I am.”

Mrs. Shane sat up in her chair all at once. “Hank, this tennis. It’s a serious hobby of yours?”

“Hobby?” Monty said. “He’ll probably be a pro someday. His brother’s getting all kinds of scholarship offers. And Hank probably will, too. Listen, Mrs. Shane, tennis is just as important to Hank as science and literature are to me.” He smiled as if he’d gotten one of his brilliant ideas. “And since Hank will probably go to college on a tennis scholarship like his brother, the tournament’s related to school!”

“Is that true, Hank? Are you planning to try for a tennis scholarship one of these days?”

I nodded.

Then a long sigh filled the room, and it was me doing the sighing. Everyone stared at me. Maybe I hadn't actually said anything, but I'd made an impact.

Mrs. Shane said slowly, "Well . . . I feel that this tennis trip might be designated as an official field trip."

Miss Caster's face got grim. "It isn't sanctioned by the school. No one but these two boys are planning to attend the event. And in Tremont's case, he isn't even going to play in the tournament. It's like taking off from school to go watch a Dodgers game. Most inappropriate."

"On the other hand," Mrs. Shane said, "I have given permission on several occasions for extended absences on the grounds that long vacations abroad would add culture to the students' lives. Perhaps if Hank and Monty were to keep diaries on the experience . . ."

"You can't mean you're comparing a tennis match to foreign trips where famous cathedrals and art museums are visited." Miss Caster's face was pink. "I feel very strongly about this, Mrs. Shane. I intend to enforce my decision of lowering these boys' grades."

Mrs. Shane's pen *tap-tap-tap*ped on her desk.

"Are you aware that Monty is under consideration for the President's Award when he completes the ninth grade? The gold, not the silver, certificate. It's something that would be in his record forever. Even one low grade would completely erase that possibility for him."

Miss Caster nodded. "In that case, he'll have to think about the repercussions and decide for himself what to do."

"I've already thought about it!" Monty burst out. "And I've decided. I'm going to Los Angeles to watch Hank and his brother play tennis. And as far as I'm concerned, you can fail me. Go ahead, if it'll make your day!"

Miss Caster opened her mouth to slam-dunk him, but Mrs. Shane held up her hand. If she'd had a whistle in her mouth, she would have looked exactly like a referee.

"You can go now, boys. I want to have a private word with Miss Caster."

At the door, I guess I amazed everyone. Even myself.

I turned back.

"I've been thinking," I said, full of that same droopy kind of depression I'd been feeling for so long now.

"Yes?" Mrs. Shane asked.

"Maybe Monty and I shouldn't go to the tournament, after all. Especially Monty. It isn't worth having his grade lowered."

Monty pinched my arm so hard, his fingers could have been a pair of pliers. "Don't listen to him, Mrs. Shane, ma'am. He's temporarily bonkers. He's not himself."

"What's the—?" Mrs. Shane began.

"Why is Hank—?" Miss Caster started to say at the same time.

"It's personal," Monty said firmly. "A horrible skeleton in the family closet. Don't even ask. And he *will be playing* in that tournament."

Both women kept their eyes on me as Monty dragged me out the door.

Once we got outside the room, he pulled me to the waiting area and shoved me into a chair before dropping into another beside me.

"I hope I wasn't wrong when I said 'temporarily.' " He glared at me. "I'm beginning to wonder about you, guy."

"And I wonder about you," I said, glaring right back at him.

"*What* do you wonder?" he snapped.

"If you've got an A-one brain in your skull, after all! You're risking the *President's Award* for a dumb *tennis tournament*? Give me a break. You think Isaac Newton gave a diddly whether some jock hit a ball over a net, except maybe it proved some theory that had a lot more to do with the universe than return versus serve?"

"Boy, you don't think we brains have an ounce of cool in us, do you, jock? In your heart of hearts, I'm still Tremont to you, aren't I?" He stuck his face right into mine. It was red, and his eyes were like bullets.

"I wasn't insulting you." I inched away from him. For the first time, I was afraid that if he threw himself on me and started punching, I might not be able to take him. It wasn't so much ferocious as crazy that he looked, but that was worse. They say that insane people are stronger than their size.

"Monty—"

"I'm going to the damn tournament." He was going to explode.

"But . . . why? Why would you risk—?"

"Because," he said. "It's . . . it's a matter of honor, don't you understand? Don't you get it that if I don't go now, if I let that—that woman"—he stabbed a finger toward the principal's office—"stop me from going to that tournament, I'll never be able to look myself in the eye again?"

His fingers clenched into fists, and I thought, Here it comes, but instead of punching me, he just said, "Even if you chicken out, Hank, even if you decide not to go to Los Angeles, *I'm* going to that tournament! I'd go to that tournament now if I hated the game of tennis! *Do you hear me?*"

I heard him all right. And my face was red, too. "What do you mean chicken out?" I blustered. "I'm just choosing grades over sports."

"Like I'd believe that in a pig's eye," Monty sneered. "That's just pure bull, buddy. You know what you're doing? You're pulling a 'poor me' trip on your parents. Turning into a real martyr."

"I am not, you creep."

"Then prove it, macho man. Tell me right now you're going to Los Angeles even if Miss Caster Oil fails you outright."

"I couldn't care less if she fails me."

"So prove it."

"Fine. I'll go play in that tournament, no matter what she says."

"Yeah?"

"Yeah. So go stick it in your ear, rabbit whiskers!" I snapped, glaring at the fuzzy hairs on his upper lip that he was trying to grow into a stupid-looking mustache.

"I'm holding you to it, chicken liver!" he said.

We turned away from each other and went to our separate corners. I mean classes. The bell had just rung and I had to go to history and he had to go to English. Miss Caster Oil, who walked through the principal's door just then, was headed in Monty's direction and would have led the way if he hadn't galloped right past her, giving her a look that was just an inch shy of thumbing his nose.

He looked back at me. "Bawwwwk, bawwk, bawwk!" he clucked. The entire hallway full of kids stared at him as he pointed straight at me.

As everyone started laughing, I kept walking in the other direction, wondering why my friend never let me off the freaking hook.

Ever.

"We heard about it, and it's awful!" Whitney said the next morning.

"It sucks frog eggs," Nick Lutazzi said.

It was right before homeroom, and a dozen kids had closed ranks around Monty and me.

"Who does that Caster creep think she is?" Marcy Webster said, giving all her attention to Monty.

Everyone knew that Monty's President's Award was being threatened by Miss Caster. And they were taking it more to heart than Monty, who said he knew who he was and didn't need any award to prove it. But I knew he'd be disappointed on the last day of school if he didn't get it. Monty wanted it, if just for his mother's sake.

"I'm asking my mom to write a letter to the principal and one to the board of education," Whitney said.

"Great idea," Nick said.

"When you think about it," Marcy said, "tennis is the same kind of extracurricular thing as band, wouldn't you say? My brother's getting two days off during the all-state band concert. I'll get my mom to write something, and maybe even my brother will write a note about it."

Pretty soon, everybody was saying they'd get their parents to write. Whitney started a petition, and her name was at the top of the list. Then came Nick, Marcy, and Sue Daniels. Then everybody grabbed for the petition. They started several sheets, with different people planning to pass them out for signatures all day.

I stood there in a daze.

"Hey, Hank?"

I turned my head, and there was Monty pushing a sheet of paper in my face. "At least you can sign your own petition," he said.

I sighed. It looked like I was going to fight for my rights, whether I wanted to or not.

"Right," I said.

I signed my name under Monty's. I wasn't in the mood to be a warrior, but I was being dragged into the arena.

By the next day, Miss Caster's life was a mess. Students wrote her notes, mothers wrote her notes, fathers and preachers wrote her notes. Somebody's aunt's boyfriend wrote her a note. Some of the notes were polite. Others were downright nasty. Somebody sent her a piece of old Limburger cheese. One of the notes, Nick Lutazzi told me, had a horrible cartoon of her looking down her hairy nose at Monty and saying, "First I will take away your President's Award, genius boy. Then I will stick you in my oven and cook you for dinner."

"Did you see it?" I asked Nick.

"Sure," he said. "I drew it."

"Oh. You made her nose hairy? Why's that? It isn't hairy in real life."

"That's what you do when somebody really ticks you off," Nick said. "You should have seen the lizard lips I gave her."

As if hairy noses and lizard lips weren't enough, Miss Caster got hooted at in the hall. Lines of people waited in the office, trying to see the principal to lodge complaints against her. So many people called the newspaper and the local news channel that by that afternoon there were reporters and a news crew in front of the school. When the last bell rang, they were on the front steps, interviewing students as we all left for the day.

Of course, they tried to make celebrities out of Monty and me. Me, the boy who was going to play in the tennis tournament. Monty, the best friend who was going to stand up for his principles and lose his President's gold certificate for skipping school to watch me play.

"Can you believe this?" Monty said after yakking his head off to the interviewer. "I found out I love cameras. Maybe I'll be in television when I grow up. An anchorman."

"If you make any more plans for yourself, bud, one adulthood won't be enough to fit everything in," I told him. Being interviewed made me nervous as all heck. I mumbled something into the microphone, and then stepped aside. You could have heard my heart pound in Toledo.

I would have run straight home, but Monty insisted we stay to watch everything. The last camera had been packed away in the van before we left. Monty waved the crew down the street and grinned like a maniac.

"Wow," he said. "We'll see ourselves on TV tonight. It'll be amazing."

"Terrific." I hoped they hadn't gotten a clear picture of my tongue. It had surely been tied in a knot.

We were on three times. Early news, regular news, and late news. It was as amazing as Monty had said it would be. There we were, standing at the big doors leading into the ninth-grade center, our friends all around us. I liked how I looked, but I didn't like the way I mumbled into the mike with my eyes staring down at my feet like I'd just stepped in something.

Monty was great though. He explained the whole situation and how it had become a matter of honor. That the President's Award was nowhere close to as important as taking a stand on this issue.

"Maybe it would be different," he said, "if Hank and I were bad students, or if we'd abused our absence privileges. Sure, the rights to extracurricular activities have to be earned. But Hank and I are good students. We haven't missed one class all year except in this grading period, and even that was because of flu. It's only common sense that we should get to miss school for a special occasion. Especially for this tournament, because Hank wants to get a tennis scholarship to college and go on to play professionally. And as Hank's tutor and best friend, I should be there, both for his sake and for a life-enriching experience that I'll never forget."

"Leave it to you to sound like a Harvard professor," I mumbled. "How can you string words together like that?"

"Shhh," five people told me. They were Monty, Jerome, Sarah, Dad, and Laura Singer. Laura and Monty had come over to watch the early news with us.

"When good students, who have no history of skipping classes, are refused their rights," Monty went on, "then . . . something is wrong."

His friends on the steps whistled like crazy and even some faculty members applauded and gave a few thumbs-up to Monty for his great performance.

The real surprise came right after that. It was the reporter's interview with Miss Caster.

She looked awful. Her eyes were full of tears, and she dabbed them away with a tissue. She explained that she had just tried to go by the rules, and the reporter said, "When you're working with teenagers, do you really think you need to keep your eye on the rule book, Miss Caster? Or shouldn't you be thinking of the kids? Don't high school kids have individual needs?"

Miss Caster's tear-filled eyes bulged, but she stuck to her guns. "Rules are rules," she said. "And that's that."

When Dad turned off the television, he shook his head. "And this woman is teaching our children," he said to Laura.

"Terrible," Laura said. "Yet, do you know, I found myself feeling sorry for her."

"That's because she isn't your teacher," Monty said. "She doesn't know the names of at least ten kids in her own class."

It was one of those statements that everyone understood. Even Sarah.

The next day, Mrs. Shane announced over the intercom that Monty and I had been cleared to go to the tennis tournament without penalty of grades. A roar went up. The whole ninth-grade center cheered. You could hear the yelling in the halls and in every nearby classroom. Everyone stomped their feet and whooped their heads off.

Everyone except Miss Caster.

Miss Caster had left the school. Someone said she was going back to her hometown in the Midwest. Somebody else said she'd gone into an insane asylum. Or maybe she was just changing school districts. Mrs. Shane probably knew what had happened to her, but she wasn't telling.

"I hate to feel we made Miss Caster run away, Monty," I said.

"I do, too, Hank," Monty said thoughtfully. "Yet it's all for the good, you know."

"You mean her disgrace?"

"Nobody forced her into disgrace. She took herself through that door, bud. Besides, she tried to disgrace you and me, didn't she? You know what I think? I think maybe Miss Caster will be a better person from this. And—who knows—a better teacher. If she decides to go on teaching, that is."

I shook my head. "Remember last night when the reporter was talking to her? She just kept talking about rules."

"Ah, well," Monty said. "Truth takes time to soak in. But when it does, it grabs hold like black hair dye."

"You know anyone who uses black hair dye?"

Just then Mrs. Shane came by, waving to us as she passed. Monty's eyes lingered on her black hair.

"I might know somebody," he said. "Not that there's anything wrong with black hair dye. Okay, bud. Now we get ready to go to L.A."

Just what I felt like doing.

11

I was stuck. We had to play the Pacific Palisades tournament. As Monty pointed out, how could we not go now after all our publicity? And it wasn't just Monty who was so intent. Jerome wanted to do it, Mom wanted us to do it, and Sarah wanted to go back to L.A. and stay with Mom for two weeks. Everyone wanted to go, except me. And maybe Dad. Ever since hearing about the couples' doubles, Dad had been keeping a very low profile. Every time I looked at him, he was frowning and rubbing the line between his eyebrows.

He didn't talk much, didn't go anywhere except to work. He and Laura Singer had begun spending some time together, but for one reason or other, Dad wasn't calling Laura now. Even worse, he'd started pacing. I could hear him in the living room way after I went to bed, *creak-creak*ing over the floorboards.

"You don't think he's gone crazy, do you?" I asked Jerome.

He shook his head, but he looked worried.

I was enough of a wreck for both of us. Even our triumph over Miss Caster didn't help my mood for long. Monty could feel my suffering and kept a tight rein on his own good spirits out of loyalty. The only thing really bothering him was how to keep to his diet on the road.

"All those dinners out," he groaned. "How am I supposed to deal with pizza? You know, we'll be eating at pizza parlors every other night if it's up to you. How am I supposed to eat at a pizza parlor and not gain weight?"

"Simple," I said. "You eat—"

"Don't tell me to eat salad while everyone else eats pizza," he begged. "I'd have to be put away."

"You'll eat pizza and salad," I explained. "Just more salad than pizza. Okay? I'll do it with you."

"Yeah?" He squared his shoulders. "If you can do it, I can do it. Do I have to use diet dressing?"

"Is there any other kind? The light vinaigrette is pretty good, actually."

"Yum," Sarah said, like she needed diet anything.

By the time we left Alamar, heading for Los

Angeles, it was almost a relief to me to hit the road. Monty showed up an hour early wearing new cargo shorts, a baggy polo shirt, and the sneakers I'd given him for Christmas. Sarah was already dressed and ready. Jerome was whistling and happy, packing his car and checking his tennis rackets. And, of course, Terri was there, all aglow, with a little bag and an extra cosmetics case. She wouldn't have missed seeing Jerome play if she had to crawl the whole way on her hands and knees. All of us except for Sarah were going to stay in adjoining rooms at the motel closest to the country club. Sarah was going straight to Mom's apartment. Everybody but me seemed happy as lunatics on a picnic.

We were in two cars with Monty and I riding with Jerome and Terri, and Sarah with Dad. I was glad to be in the teenagers' car, because Jerome and Terri kept talking the whole way, which meant I didn't have to. They were excited about being at Stanford together next year and about all the brochures that had just come through the mail. Every once in a while, Jerome would reach over and squeeze Terri's hand and they'd smile at each other.

It all gave me a terrible headache. I wished Dog could be with us, but he had to spend the next two weeks with Terri's parents, who were thrilled to have such a sweet pup in their household, even though they'd been warned about the furniture and the rugs.

"Just win the tournament," Terri's mom said to Jerome. Then she said it to me, too.

If Terri's going to be like her mom, she'll be a nice woman. She'll also have a nice figure, which was something I was already secretly noticing about Terri now that she'd started wearing prettier clothes. She was changing right before my eyes.

Monty looked at me collapsed in my corner against the door.

"Who plays first?" he said. "You or Jerome?"

"Me," I told him. "They work from the bottom up."

"Oh," he said. "That makes sense."

"Your practices have been uninspired lately, Hank," Jerome said from the front seat. "To put it mildly. Think you'll be all right?"

That made me straighten in my seat. I hadn't been putting my heart into my workouts. It hadn't worried me much. But now I found myself hoping I wasn't going to make a freaking idiot of myself in front of the serious tennis world.

"Maybe you could volley with me for a while when we get in?" I muttered.

"I could do that." Jerome looked at me over his shoulder. He was smiling.

* * *

By the time we checked into the motel, I was moving in a dream. Something awful had happened to my brain. It felt as muddled as it had during that first week of algebra with Miss Caster.

Monty was running around checking the TV and getting a bucket of ice cubes and a couple of Cokes from the vending machine. Part of me was unpacking clothes and putting stuff in drawers and part of me was thinking about Dad, Jerome, Terri, Monty, and me being in one part of town, and Sarah and Mom being somewhere else. I kept seeing my family the way it once was, all together. Like a whole thing, rather than a jigsaw puzzle with pieces missing.

I made myself remember the bad stuff, too, not just the good. Mom crying in her bedroom. Dad pacing, like he'd been doing lately. Maybe that's what had reminded me so much of the past, that pacing of his. I remembered all the awful silences. The way Jerome would slam in and out of doors. How timid Sarah was in those days, jumping if you looked at her wrong. And that terrible feeling in my own chest, the worrying about who was going to say what to set the other one off.

For the first time ever, I thought: Maybe it's better this way.

The thought drilled a hole in my stomach. Because even knowing that it was better with Mom and Dad divorced, I still wanted us all together again. Was that a crazy thought or what? That you'd rather put your family back together, even if everybody was happier being apart.

Monty was watching me. I could feel him knowing what I was thinking. He's got radar in his brain.

"Do you ever wish your dad would come home?" I asked him. Monty hardly ever mentions his father, even though he talks about most everything, *especially* stuff that goes deep.

Monty gasped when I said that, as if he'd just dived into cold water.

"No," he said. His voice was flatter than I'd ever heard it.

"You don't want to be a family again?"

"I *am* a family," he said. "My mom and I are a family. Listen, Hank, it's different with me than with you. Your parents are both nice people. My dad . . . well, he has his problems, that's all. Maybe it's not his fault. Maybe he shouldn't have married and had a kid. It's like he's all wrapped up in himself. I don't think my dad even remembers he has a kid most of the time."

"Monty, I'm sorry, I—"

"Don't be all *that* sorry. We weren't talking about me, anyhow. Listen, Hank, trying to put a marriage back together is harder than figuring out quantum theory. Which isn't so hard, really," he added thoughtfully. "I don't get why people say quantum theory is so—"

"What do you know about any quantum theory?" I interrupted.

"I've read a couple of physics books." He shrugged. "Just for the fun of it."

"For the fun of it?"

I hit him with a pillow.

"We have time for a swim before we head to the club," I said. Maybe a swim would clear my head, but I doubted it. Absolutely nothing seemed to work.

"Swimming—great," Monty said, enthusiastic in a flash. "I've got a new suit. Like yours—your quick-dry Viking brand."

"It doesn't ride down your belly?"

He grinned. "I don't have much of a belly anymore, remember?"

"Oh, yeah. I won't have to ask you to act like you don't know me then." Even Monty's outie belly button wasn't so outie anymore, now that the fat wasn't pushing it from the inside out. But I couldn't even take the usual satisfaction out of that thought. I was just strung too tight.

"Hurry up," I told him as he looked for his earplugs. "I'm hot."

Monty turned around and looked at me. "You know why you're nervous, Hank?"

"Who said I was nervous?"

He ignored me. "You're nervous because ever since the divorce, you've felt alone."

"Baloney," I muttered.

"What you don't realize, Hank, is that you'll have a lot of people with you on the court. Including your mom and dad. We'll all be out there with you."

"Thanks, guy, but they only allow two players. Me on my side and my opponent on the other."

"You don't get it—" he started.

"*You're* going to get it, *pow,* right in the chops, if you don't step on it."

"Okay," he grumbled. "But I think I'm on to something."

I was on my way out the door. It was only the middle of April, and L.A. was already in a heat wave. Me, too. I was way too overheated for Monty's philosophy.

My first practice that afternoon went like you might expect—lousy.

"Where's your form, little brother?" Jerome yelled at me from across the net. "You're hobbling around over there. Come *on* already! You're too far back! Too far into the baseline! Off balance! What's the matter with your feet? Are they nailed to the court?"

"No, they're moving," I said. "I'll get there."

"You could fool me. Come on, Hank, you're playing like an old man!" he shouted.

"Why don't you just yell it out?" I muttered. "There's a few people in Pacific Palisades who didn't hear you."

It was going even worse than my most horrible nightmare. Everywhere I looked, I saw players I'd known for years and hoped they weren't watching me practice. They should have seen me just a few weeks ago. I was terrific then. You couldn't tell it now. If I played like this tomorrow in my first game, I would have to wear a bag over my head.

"Hank!" Mom called from the bleachers. "You're not bringing who you are to your game. You're so much better than you're letting us see."

I wasn't sure about that. That day when Jerome and I had chewed up the Cool Dude twins seemed like a hundred years ago. Right now, I could hardly hold on to my tennis racket.

Sure enough, Jerome hit a hard one to my

backhand, and my racket flew out of my hand and halfway across the court.

"HANK!" My brother and my mother both screamed at me with one voice. In stereo.

"O-*kay,* I'm ready to give it a better shot now!" I hopped after the racket. "I was just warming up before."

"If that's your warm-up," Mom said, "we'd better work on it."

"Yeah," Jerome said. "And until you improve it, I never want to see you warm up in public again!"

I took up my racket and hoped those two cute girls on the bleachers weren't giggling at me.

"I'm ready," I said. "Come on, Jerome, hit me a hot one. I'm on top of it."

Unfortunately, tennis isn't a game of talk. You have to be able to actually hit the ball. And Jerome's hot one flew past me like it had wings. I never even saw it.

As Monty says, "Truth is truth." And the truth was, those two cute girls were definitely giggling at me.

"Why don't I just give up?" I mumbled.

"What?" yelled my mom.

"I said I'll never give up!"

"Good guy! You'll get there!"

Maybe. But would I be alive?

That night, we went out for spareribs. I felt like a sparerib. At least, I was aware of all my bones. And they all ached. It didn't make any sense to me. It wasn't like I was out of practice.

"There's practice and there's practice," Jerome said, giving me the evil eye. "It was pretty obvious on the court today that you were, well, let's just say 'missing form.' "

"Are you telling me that even the club lifeguard knows I'm off my game?"

"Even the woman that pins on the name tags. Even the waiters in the dining room."

Monty said, "The problem is, you're so mentally gummed up that the gunk in your brain has oozed right into your bones, Hank."

Dad looked at me over the huge beef rib he was eating. He asked me if I thought I'd be all right to play tomorrow.

"Are you kidding?" I said. "I'll be a real killer out there."

It came out of my mouth like a little cross baby whimper.

Everybody looked at me. Wearing their big

white bibs, holding their spareribs, all with these big pitying eyes, they made me think of surgeons getting ready to operate on a hopeless case.

"Hank," Terri breathed. She looked like she was getting ready to cry.

"One thing we know you're not going to be, anyhow," Monty said, digging me in the side with his elbow.

"What's that?"

"An actor."

If I hadn't been feeling so terrible, I'd have scheduled a weighted sock fight with him for later. As it was, I just groaned. I blushed as I noticed Terri still staring at me like I was the most pathetic thing she'd seen since old broccoli.

"Listen," I said. "I'm one hundred percent o-*kay*. Does everybody understand that?"

For a minute, nobody said a word. Then Dad said, "Sure, Hank. We understand."

"Sure we do," Terri said, and Jerome and Monty nodded.

It was about the sorriest group of understanding eyes I'd ever hoped to see. I could only hope I wasn't going to have to look into eyes like that after my match tomorrow.

12

It was late afternoon the next day when I made my first appearance in a Palisades country club competition in almost a year. I was nervous as a cat. Even after Jerome had volleyed with me and bullied me into better form, and even after Mom had taken over where he left off, practically losing her voice yelling at me, I still wasn't back to my best stuff.

"Good thing you're playing Troy Clark," Jerome said. "You might still have a chance."

Troy Clark was pathetic by my standards. At least, by my old standards. I'd known him for years and seldom lost even a game to him. If I couldn't beat Troy, I'd just as soon hang it up.

"He looks bigger than he did last year," I said as Jerome escorted me up to the court like an anxious mother hen. Mom gave me a nervous wave from the other side of the court.

"Troy's big, all right," Jerome agreed, "but he still can't play tennis. He's yours for the taking, bro. Go get him."

Troy raised his racket to me as I walked onto the court, and grinned like he was pleased to be playing me.

"Yo, Hank! What hole have you been hiding in these days?"

I only wished I had a hole handy just then. It was time to do a practice volley. I looked at Jerome one last time. Even while he was giving me a thumbs-up, I could see it plain as day: My brother was afraid I was going to lose to Troy Clark.

I couldn't stop shaking as Troy took his place behind the service line.

Come on, I ordered myself. Get it together already. You can't let yourself turn green right here in front of everybody. And it's Troy, for Pete's sake. Troy. The same old Troy that never won a match in his life. Sarah could beat him. Come on, guy. You can do this.

Sure enough, Troy's first serve came over the net like a cream puff, just waiting to be flattened by my racket.

I hit it into the net.

The groans of the crowd made me feel worse. Even Troy looked disgusted with me.

Great, I told myself. Your life hasn't been horrible enough, you're going to add humiliation to the heap.

The first three games went to Troy by default. I couldn't seem to show up for the match. At least, I hoped that wasn't me out there lousing up every return, every serve, every volley, like the Genius of Flop. I was going down big time. On the sidelines, Mom's face was whiter than I'd ever seen it before, with awful little red specks here and there. It was like her blood vessels had started to pop, one by one.

But destiny is destiny.

It was Troy who pulled me out of the hole I'd started to dig for myself in the first part of the match. As long as I had known Troy, he had been an unenthusiastic player, goaded into play by his parents and really longing to play football, which neither of his folks would permit. He looked like he wanted to lose our match more than he'd wanted anything in his life, and the way I was playing, it took every ounce of his determination to make his dream come true.

"You're getting there, Hank!" Jerome shouted from the bleachers.

"Hang in there, Hank!" Monty yelled.

As I heard Sarah's excited scream, I thought that maybe I was going to pull this thing off after all.

It was the wrong thing to think. Right away, I started hitting balls out of bounds, into the net, into the crowd. Flop sweat had set in again.

"Hank!" my mother yelled, both arms in a stranglehold around Sarah's neck. "Stop thinking so much! Keep your eyes on the ball!"

What was she, a mind reader? She'd caught me thinking?

"Breathe!" Mom commanded.

I looked at the front row and saw her there. Both her hands swept up and out from her diaphragm as if she were trying to breathe for me.

"Come on, Hank," she said again. "You can do it!"

Beside her, little Sarah was breathing, too.

There was an awful sinking feeling in my stomach, but I breathed. In the stands, Dad was breathing right along with me. Monty was next to him, breathing and wringing his hands. Then Terri—almost hyperventilating. Jerome, shoulders moving up and down . . . breathing.

And in those few seconds, I got what Monty meant when he said I wouldn't be alone on the court. I could almost feel him telling me: *See, Hank? All of us are here for you. Your mom and dad, too. Everybody's right here, rooting you on.*

If that was really true, then all those years of

training with Mom, of Dad cheering me on, still made sense. The divorce didn't mean those years weren't important. I still had people who cared.

"Now concentrate," Mom said in a softer voice that only I and maybe a hundred other people could hear.

So I took another deep breath and let it all go. Then I glared at the ball until it grew from the size of a pea into a grape. And from a grape into an apple. Pretty soon it was a cantaloupe, and finally it was a big fat juicy watermelon.

I smashed it with everything I had.

It seemed like a minute later that somehow I was walking toward the net, the victor, and Troy was coming up beside me to sling his arm around my shoulders.

"Thanks," he said as we walked toward the judge's chair to shake hands.

"For what?" I did a double take at the sight of his beaming face.

"A loss in the first round means I'll be allowed to play in the spring jamboree," Troy explained. Seeing that I was lost, he added, "Football. I tried out in the fall, and coach said I made quarterback, then my folks wouldn't let me play. When they saw how miserable I was, they finally said if I washed out again here, they'd change their minds. Thanks, Hank."

"Glad I could help out," I mumbled. But I was feeling better. I was starting to remember who I used to be. Or maybe I was remembering who I wanted to be.

That night, everyone but Dad had dinner with Mom. She took us to the best Italian restaurant in the Palisades, and I told Monty to start off with a mountain of salad to fill up a little, to put a hold on the bread, and then to eat all the pasta he wanted. This night only, I warned.

He got so into eating, he hardly talked, so you know what the meal meant to him.

"Listen," Mom said all at once. "I've got some great news. I've accepted a full-time job at the country club. Starting next fall, I'm not going to be on the road anymore, except for a few key tournaments like the Grand Slam. I'm going to be able to spend a lot more time with you."

Jerome looked at her. "Is this something you really want? Or is it because you want to please us?"

Her eyes swept over the table, taking in Jerome, Sarah and me, and Monty and Terri, too.

"I want it for me," she said. "I want it for you, too, Jerry. For all of us."

She was looking directly at me now, like maybe I most of all needed to hear what she was trying to tell us. Her gaze was soft and full of what she felt and what I wouldn't let her say to me these days.

It was full of love.

Our mom loved us enough to change the focus of her life. Not totally so that she'd lose herself, like she'd talked about to us sometimes, but to change it enough so that she could see more of us. She was trying her hardest to be a person who had enough time with her kids.

"Jerry." Mom's voice shook as she looked over at my brother now. "Have you been thinking about what you'll do next year?"

"Yes," Jerome said.

She looked at him for a long time. "Maybe I've been looking forward so much to having you back in L.A. and getting you ready for the circuit that I forgot to ask you what you want for yourself. Do you really want to go on the pro circuit after high school? Somehow, I think you'd rather go to college. Have you applied to any?"

He looked back at her. "I've applied to Stanford."

"I see. If that's what you want—"

"I've been thinking, Mom. I want an education, but I also want a shot at the circuit. There aren't many years in a pro's life."

"No," she said carefully. "Not many."

"But I think," he said hurriedly, "that if I play tennis at Stanford for two years, and if things go well, then I could go straight to the circuit from there. That way I'd be closer to a degree and I'd still have time to try my hand at the pros. I could get my degree later. What do you think?"

She looked like she was having trouble breathing. "Has Stanford offered you a scholarship?"

He grinned at her. "You should know better than anyone. Stop playing innocent. You sent them a tape. You sent them my stats. They showed up on the campus two weeks ago, and I played two matches with a pro they brought along. Yeah, Mom. They offered me the scholarship."

She cried then, opening her arms to him. "Jerry," she said. It was all she could get out.

I was glad to be there for that moment. In fact, I was glad that Terri was there, too. And Monty, of course. His eyes were lit up like lightbulbs. He's a connoisseur of what he calls the wine of life.

This was one of those times.

Two days later, I made a better show of it on the courts, and my match after that was even better. My heart had come back, and my form wasn't too shabby either. I won the next match in straight sets and went on to the quarterfinals. Jerome was marching along right behind me, trying not to get complacent with his game. When everyone keeps comparing you to Sampras, mental toughness gets to be as much a problem as mechanics.

Because Jerome was born humble, he had a good grip on things.

Quarterfinals were not a lark. I found myself against Mark Anderson, the best in my age group. I came up against Mark early, because my year off the local amateur circuit had dropped me in seeding. Otherwise, I really believe we'd have met in the finals, playing for the championship.

We went at each other with all we had, with the bleachers screaming for us, and it wasn't a half-bad feeling. Even when I missed a point, I knew I was playing the best tennis I'd ever played in my life and against the best player, except for Jerome, that I'd ever played.

My net game was there, like I'd spent all winter practicing for with Jerome. My backhand was as solid as it should have been, probably because day after day, Jerome had made me play whole sets, all to the backhand. The only trouble was that Mark's backhand was there, too, and his net game must have been learned on Murderer's Row. He won the first set with a two-game margin, but I pulled off an upset in a second-set tiebreaker. The third set went to another tiebreaker, and Mark won it when my lob flew over his head and went out of bounds by about half an inch.

By that time, my shirt was stuck to my back, and Mark's shirt was so wet he changed it between sets. And we just kept on playing.

I got on a streak the next set and broke his serve early on, then managed to hold serve straight through for a win, pulling even in sets. It could have been anybody's match then, except that Mark's solid year of tournament play boosted him just a notch above me, even though I'd had the advantage of practicing with Jerome. The last set finally went in Mark's favor, but I could tell one thing for sure—he knew he'd been playing tennis.

After it was over, and Mark had won our match, advancing to the semifinals, the crowd cheered for both of us, and Mark told me I was the best he'd ever played in his age group and that he hoped we'd play each other as pros one day.

The world got fuzzy when he said that, and I took the possibility of it straight to my heart. Mom happened to come up right as I was thinking it, and without even realizing what I was saying, I told her my thought. That someday Jerome and I might both be pros, playing on the circuit together.

She looked at me and said, "Hank, the way you

played today, it can happen. I know it can. Dare to have the dream. If I can teach my children only that one thing, then I've succeeded."

Monty just grabbed me and hugged. I'd have told him to get stuffed, but there are times when sentimental saps should be allowed some free rein. Since Jerome did the same thing, and Terri and Dad, too, what could a future pro do? Even little Sarah stared up at me goggle-eyed like she'd just gotten another hero besides Jerome and Dad.

All of a sudden, life had a kind of shine to it.

Two days later, Jerome played the finals in his age group.

When he walked onto the court, an unbelievable thing happened. People all over the place started applauding. Some of them even stood up. I'd never seen that happen at the country club. Afterward, yes, especially when the play had been great, but never before the match even started. But the way Jerome had been playing all week was amazing, and I guess people just wanted to say thank you. Maybe they felt grateful to be in on the beginning of what promised to be a really great career.

"Oh, no," Mom groaned, digging her nails into my shoulder. "This is not good. This is pressure. Jerome may feel like he has to play differently or something to earn all those accolades. It could throw him off. Way off."

"Jerome has changed quite a bit this year, Mom," I said, looking at him unscrewing his racket from its frame. He wasn't smiling or frowning. It was hard to imagine what he was thinking. He was in his own world.

Mom was looking at him, too. Suddenly she smiled, but there were tears in her eyes. "You mean he's grown up some, don't you?"

"Yeah, I guess that's exactly what I mean." My brother stretched out, and then jogged in place for a while, getting his feet going. Somewhere over the year, he'd picked up a couple of inches, bringing him up to six three and counting. "He looks really good to me. I don't think anything will shake him up, Mom."

She blinked her tears away. "You know what? I think I've worried enough about you guys. I'm holding you back. I'm being suffocating. It's because I haven't spent enough time with you."

"Sure you have," I said.

She looked at me. "What do you mean, Hank? I haven't been there with you to—"

"You *have* been," I interrupted. "You call us almost every day, you send those dumb little cards to us, you spend every minute you're not working in a town you don't have much interest in just so you can see us. You didn't leave us at all, Mom. And now you've changed your whole life to be with us even more."

Now she couldn't even blink the tears away. They just kept coming.

"Then you know that I—" she started to say, but the words got strangled in her throat.

"That you love us," I said. "Yeah, yeah, yeah. *We know* already. We *know*. Give it a rest, for Pete's sake."

We both laughed.

By then Jerome was volleying with Bobby Montgomery.

"Bobby'll never beat Jerome," I said confidently.

"Why's that?" Mom asked. "Bobby's *good*."

"With a name like Bobby Montgomery, he's going to play pro tennis?"

"With a name like Jerome, your brother's going to play pro tennis?"

"You've dropped the Jerry, haven't you?" I said, smiling at her.

"Everyone else did. Gotta go with the flow."

"Does every adult say that?"

"Huh?"

"Never mind," I said. "Actually, I think Jerome is a neat name for a tennis star. I'm not kidding. It sounds famous to me."

My mother started trembling, and I knew the match was about to begin. To distract her, I pointed up at Terri, who was gazing at my brother with gaga eyes, and said, "What do you think of his girlfriend, Mom?"

Our mother's face lit up. "Imagine Jerome picking out a girl who's going to go into sports medicine! Amazing, yes?"

"Sports medicine?" I said and almost asked, "What happened to being a psychiatrist?" Good old Terri, I thought.

Okay, so it was Jerome all over the place. The Cool Dude twins had been just a dress rehearsal. Today was the day that Jerome really returned to his true destiny, with all the people he'd been with for so long on the amateur circuit there to see it happen. It seemed right to me that our whole gang came down to sit close to where I was sitting beside Mom.

Well, Dad was one row up, but who was counting?

Was Jerome good? He tore up the court. He had Bobby Montgomery talking to himself. The Stanford people had come to see him play and just about broke their arms patting one another on the back for landing him, especially when Jerome made it clear to them after the match that he wasn't about to renege on the scholarship and go pro all at once.

Our section of the bleachers had some very happy people. Mark Anderson had come to watch the finals of Jerome's match after winning his own championship. He sat between Monty and me like the three of us had suddenly become best friends, and he was cheering for Jerome as hard as anybody else. After all, Jerome was kind of a symbol of where Mark and I wanted to go in our own careers.

"The thing that's nice about the tennis world," I explained to Monty, "is that it's like one big extended family."

Monty grinned at me as Jerome took the trophy and held it up for all to see. "The whole *world's* like that, Hank. We're all family."

I couldn't argue with him.

With the singles matches finished in all age classes, now there were only the doubles left to play. Starting with Jerome and me. We chewed up the court when we took the brothers' doubles. The Synch was on.

It was more than fun. "Sweet" is the word. Man, it was sweet.

I figured that Whitney would ask me how I'd done when I got back to Alamar. Now I could tell her we'd won. Not that I'd say much about it. Unless she really pressed me for the details, that is. Whitney is the kind of girl who gets interested in details.

After our championship cup presentation—twin cups, one for each brother—we stuck around to watch the rest of the doubles tournament. Until we got to the couples' doubles, I was glad we'd stayed. But watching the first two matches with all those smiling couples gave me a pain in my head.

Or to be honest, a pain in my heart.

I was so lost in my own thoughts, I didn't hear the announcement of the next couples match. Then Monty poked me hard in the back, and Jerome put his arm across my shoulders while Sarah shrieked and Terri just sat there crying. When I looked up, I didn't even believe what I was seeing.

Mom and Dad were walking out on the court together. They were smiling and joking and pretending to bean each other with their rackets.

I'd dreamed of that moment all winter long, and now that it was happening, I didn't know what to feel. It was, as Monty would have said, overwhelming. Looking at my parents play together and kid each other and win their match against the other couple was something out of a dream.

The only thing I could think of was that our parents loved us more than anything in the universe. Because seeing them on the court together, I realized nothing was ever so clear to me in my life than that they weren't the normal couple anymore and never were going to be. They were a different sort of couple now—people who loved their kids enough to swallow their differences and to hang in there together. To find a way to keep being friends after they'd quit being married to each other.

"Sometimes," Monty said, leaning closer to me, "I could envy you, Hank."

How could you say anything back to that, when you knew what your best friend was feeling and you also knew it could never come true for him? Not with a father who never even bothered to call at Christmas and didn't pay his child support. Not with a father who didn't even remember he had a son most of the time.

I slung my arm over his shoulders.

"I could envy me, too, buddy," I said softly.

As I told Dog, "Life isn't too shabby, if you give it your best shot."

School is almost over for the year, and Jerome and Terri are getting ready to go to college. I can't even imagine what it's going to be like without the two of them hanging around the house all the time. I guess we'll find a way to make it work. At least Monty is still right next door.

Dad and Laura Singer have been spending more time together, talking about mortgages, home maintenance, and the petition that's circulating for replacing the septic tanks in our neighborhood with a new sewer.

Monty's a little disappointed that for all their talking, they aren't actually dating or anything. He finally admitted to me he'd had a dream where my dad married his mom and we all lived together in a bigger house by the ocean with a tennis court out back.

"And when did you hope all this might happen?" I asked him.

"Hopefully, by August," he said.

We both laughed a little at that. On the other hand, stranger things have happened. I just read about a guy who met his wife while she was putting new shingles on his roof. If that can happen, maybe our parents can notice each other over the septic tank problem.

Dog looked at me as I was explaining it all to him, and in dog language he reminded me not to get too high on everything, that certain disappointments are built into the very fabric of life.

For example, he said, I'm not ever going to be a sheepdog. It's just not going to happen, guy, no matter how much I don't want to disappoint you.

"The funny thing is," I told him, "dreams change. For example, you. I don't even want you to be a sheepdog anymore. I saw one the other day and it was a big ugly dirty thing with its hair all matted and stuff stuck to its behind. It didn't walk, it waddled, that's how sloppy fat it was. Actually, I sort of like your being a cute little peek-a-poo, if you want to know."

He got this look in his eyes like some big weight had just dropped off his back, and he licked my face. Of course, he always licks my face, but this was something special.

"You see, Dog," I went on, "the way life works is that we meet people along the way, and if we bring the best of who we are to them and they do the same to us, they start being like family. After that, there's no way to get them out of our hearts. It doesn't matter what we look like, or what we've been like for the rest of our lives until we met. We change each other, and accept each other, and even if everything doesn't work out exactly the way you wish it would, we all get by together."

This is true.

Things are going pretty well right now. Monty's a shoo-in for the gold President's Award. As for me, I expect to be on the honor roll for the last term. After that, we'll say good-bye to the ninth-grade center and get ready for the main campus. Whitney says she's nervous about walking onto that campus as a sophomore. Monty says come the fall, we're probably all going to feel real important for a while.

For Jerome and Sarah and me, it just feels good that our parents aren't killing each other anymore, and are even friends. Now when Mom calls us, she always asks to speak to Dad and pretty soon the two of them are laughing together. It reminds me of something Dad once said right after they split up. He said that the worst part of it was losing my Mom's friendship, because they'd had that before they were ever in love with each other. Now they've got back part of what they lost.

For now, Monty and I just wonder how we're going to fill the summer. There isn't much to do in Alamar. No rock concerts, no amusement parks, not many movies. There's only one miniature golf course in town, and it's a shabby-looking piece of goods, I'll tell you. Nick Lutazzi wants me to show him how to play tennis. So does Whitney. I gave her one lesson and the way she looks in a tennis skirt,

I'd swear she was born for the game. All in all, life is pretty cool right now. I guess I can take it on.

Hey, when you're a tennis ace, you don't need much but a court, a net, a few tennis balls, and a racket. And a friend to volley with. And a dog to chase the stray balls.

After that, you're home free.